About the Author

Jill Yielder, PhD, is a Jungian analyst and psychotherapist working in private practice, as well as working in the medical programme at the University of Auckland. While she has published a wide range of non-fiction articles relating to higher education, psychology and health and wellbeing, this is her first novel. She lives in Auckland, New Zealand.

Through the Labyrinth

Jill Yielder

Through the Labyrinth

Olympia Publishers
London

www.olympiapublishers.com
OLYMPIA PAPERBACK EDITION

Copyright © Jill Yielder 2021

The right of Jill Yielder to be identified as author of
this work has been asserted in accordance with sections 77 and 78
of the Copyright, Designs and Patents Act 1988.

All Rights Reserved

No reproduction, copy or transmission of this publication
may be made without written permission.
No paragraph of this publication may be reproduced,
copied or transmitted save with the written permission of the
publisher, or in accordance with the provisions
of the Copyright Act 1956 (as amended).

Any person who commits any unauthorised act in relation to
this publication may be liable to criminal
prosecution and civil claims for damage.

A CIP catalogue record for this title is
available from the British Library.

ISBN: 978-1-80074-109-6

This is a work of fiction.
Names, characters, places and incidents originate from the writer's
imagination. Any resemblance to actual persons, living or dead, is
purely coincidental.

First Published in 2021

Olympia Publishers
Tallis House
2 Tallis Street
London
EC4Y 0AB

Printed in Great Britain

Acknowledgements

Special thanks to Andrew, Rachael and Christine, for their support, advice and editing. Thanks to Rachael for a wonderful sketch of my grandmother's bas relief plate, and to Andrew for drawing the map.

Disclaimer

It is inevitable when working in a diverse psychotherapeutic practice, that snippets of stories I've been told over years will find their way into my writing. However, there are no aspects of this novel that are true, or have been taken from an individual patient/client's clinical material. The novel is entirely a work of fiction, drawing on my understanding of the world and the psychology of people in it; the patterns of interaction that occur, the effects of trauma, and the experiences, good and bad, that people find themselves having to cope with to make sense of the world. Names, characters, places, events and incidents are either the products of my imagination or used in a fictitious manner. Any resemblance to actual persons, living or dead, or actual events is purely coincidental.

At the still point of the turning world.
Neither flesh nor fleshless;
Neither from nor towards; at the still point,
there the dance is,
But neither arrest nor movement.
And do not call it fixity,
Where past and future are gathered.
Neither movement from nor towards,
Neither ascent nor decline.
Except for the point, the still point,
There would be no dance,
and there is only the dance.

T. S. Elliott, Burnt Norton, 1936

For Dale
Namaste

Preface

Stories bring people together. Through stories we can connect to experiences or feelings and explore them as if they were our own, finding a sense of connection from a 'safe' distance, allowing them to percolate in our psyche. We don't have to do anything other than read or listen, just absorb the story and grow our understanding through the effect the story has on us.

This story can be read two ways: either as an adventure story; or by older readers who may be interested in psychology, as an allegory to illustrate the tasks that a person, regardless of gender, may need to undertake psychologically in order to find a sense of wholeness. Because of this, some readers may wish to read 'A Jungian perspective for the older reader' found at the end of the book, as a guide to the psychological meaning of the tale, either before reading it, or leave it to the end and just enjoy the story!

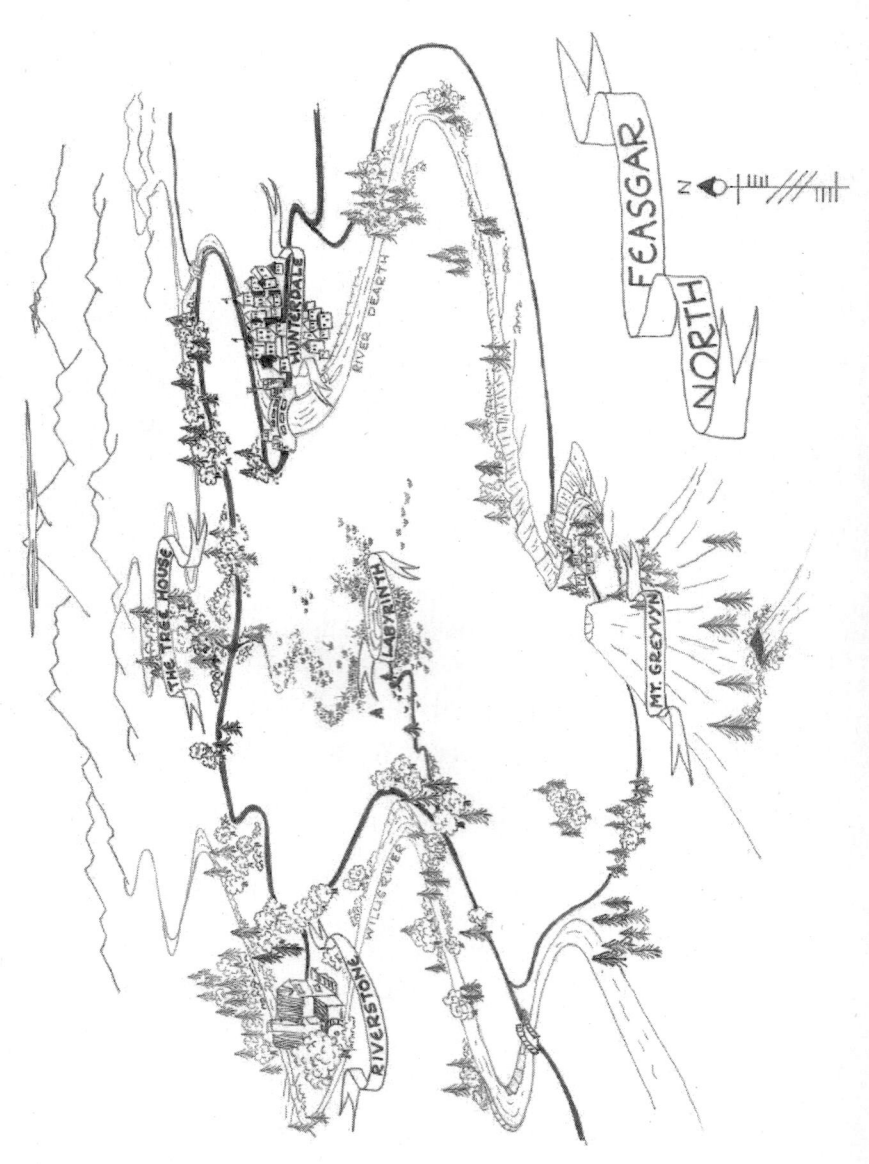

Prologue

A woman, looking intense and drawn, long hair awry, stared at the pottery wheel in front of her, where the clay was transforming from a sullen lump into a circular shape. Hands sliding and shaping, grooves forming, moving around and around, mesmerising. She was muttering to herself. Had anyone been listening they may have heard snatches of her thoughts mumbled aloud over the sound of the relentless click and swish of the wheel rhythmically turning. Maybe something like:

'Ah, here you are, at last, just as I was promised. Two lovely young ones from opposite sides of the world. The boy with a dark wedge in his heart — he's had trust and love shattered inside him. Wonderful ingredients to work with. And the fair girl, so sweet, so lovely... Will she find some mettle? Will they succeed at their task? Will I get what I need this time, or will they go the same way as all the others...? Not long to wait now...'

She came out of her reverie and looked down to see that she had created something that looked like a gaping mouth, with grimacing lips and a dark void beyond. She angrily smashed her fist into the clay and it collapsed back into a shapeless lump.

Chapter I
The Mill on the River

Sarah was curled up comfortably in an old, over-stuffed and blousy armchair at her grandparents' place, feeling warm and drowsy. The sound of the crackling fire was soothing, and she gazed dreamily at the flickering embers as they climbed up the chimney like red-tongued dragons. She'd been staying with them for two days now and had spent today outside with her grandfather helping him around the property — stacking firewood, cleaning the paths before the snow came, and talking. Talking about anything and everything — he was so easy to be with — the plants, the trees, the smells of the woods nearby, her friends, what she wanted to learn when she was a bit older at school. She'd been feeling more and more lately that this was her safe place, but she still hadn't managed to bring up the biggest thing on her mind — the real reason she was staying with them.

Sarah had a hollow feeling in her stomach, a mix of confusion and worry. Everything seemed to have changed. She wasn't enjoying school like she used to. She had one best friend, Hannah, but she'd been travelling in Europe with her parents for the last four weeks and while she was away, Sarah didn't know what to do with herself at school. There was a bunch of girls in the popular group — part of her would like to hang out with them, just because they seemed to have fun, but at the same time they were mean, making fun of other girls, like about how they looked. Sarah didn't like that and she knew that it was likely that they made fun of her too behind her back, not because of how she looked — she knew she was quite pretty, well Hannah said she was anyway. She did really well at school though and she knew that some of the girls were jealous of her, but at the same time some of the group wanted to cosy up to her and Hannah because they made up interesting things to do. The other girls who weren't in the popular group mostly hung around the edges of whatever was happening and, although she knew it was big-headed, she thought most of them were a bit boring. So, without Hannah to hang out with, she wandered around pretty much on her own, doing things like going to the library where she could bury herself in a book and no one would notice she was a loner.

Lunch times were a nightmare! The food was provided by the school and everyone had to sit together to eat in the dining room. If she got there with everyone else, she had to make the agonising decision of where to sit — should she try to sit with the popular girls, join up with one of the uncool girls, or try to find a space by herself and identify as a loner? If she rushed and got there early, she could find a table and sit with her head down and see what happened, but it was horrible when girls walked right past, obviously not wanting to sit with her... Why didn't the other girls seem to get screwed up about everything like she did?

And something funny was going on at home. Her parents were so wrapped up in themselves it was as if she didn't really exist.

Like, a few weeks ago she'd felt really unwell when she'd been helping her mum do some painting at her dad's work. Her mum seemed too busy and stressed to take much notice until she got really dizzy and nearly fainted. After that, she took her home and dropped her off at the house without even going in with her to make sure she was okay. They found her when they returned home several hours later, collapsed on the floor just inside the front door with a really high fever — she was delirious for the next couple of days and couldn't remember anything other than feeling like she was burning up, that something was inside her, taking her over, trying to consume her arms and chest and neck. Since then, she'd been tearful and sort of wobbly, and battling with a feeling of not being cared for.

There was an enormous amount of tension in the house — it was like they were all walking on eggshells, trying not to crush them. It felt like all the unsaid, maybe even unthought-of, things between her parents were stretched out taut like the rubber of a catapult, just waiting to be fired. And now, suddenly, that had happened... wham, it was all let go of; all those things were launched at each other two days ago, and Sarah had watched, terrified, as both her parents had said horrible things to hurt each other. And she'd felt totally helpless, unable to do anything to stop them.

Her grandmother suddenly came into the room, dragging her out of her spiralling thoughts. "Here you are — I've brought you a mug of hot chocolate. You look cosy. Are you all right sitting here on your own? Your granddad will be in soon." Sarah's grandmother was a slim woman in her seventies, with grey, shoulder-length hair caught up in combs just behind her ears, little tucks of skin around her neck giving away her age — she didn't have the round grandmotherly, kindly sort of presence like Hannah's gran, and she wore clothes that were always very neat and tidy as if she was still going to work every day. She and her grandfather had both been doctors in the local village until they retired a few years ago.

"Yes thanks, Gran. I'm just enjoying the fire."

"What's that you're reading?"

"'The Song of the Lioness', by Tamora Pierce. You should read it. Mum really likes her books, though she doesn't seem to have much time for them at the moment. I used to read out loud to her in the kitchen while she was cooking dinner."

"Oh? So how come you don't do that any more?"

"I don't know. Things are just… different." Sarah felt bad talking about it out loud, as if somehow, she was being disloyal to her parents. Besides, if she kept it to herself, maybe it would turn out okay and no one would need to know what had been happening. Maybe they just needed a break from her. She didn't think she made things difficult for them, but if they had space, they might sort it out. She wondered how much her grandparents knew anyway, since she'd been left with them so abruptly, but neither of them gave any indication that her mum had talked to them.

Her grandmother squatted down beside her chair. "Sarah, remember your grandad and I are here for you whenever you need us. We love having you here." She patted her on the knee, a little awkwardly, and left the room.

Sarah loved her gran, but she seemed to find it difficult to show affection, a bit like her mum, though she guessed she did it through baking things for her and, like now, making a point of checking she was okay. Her grandad, though, gave her wonderful hugs. He felt really big and safe, and somehow made her feel really special and worth talking and listening to. As for her dad... well she didn't see a lot of him. He was always working, and when he got home, he seemed worn out. When she was little, they'd had holidays together at the beach or in the Lake District. Once they'd been to Scotland, to Oban and then across to Iona, which was really bleak and at the same time totally magical. They'd been promising for ages to take her to Paris, but it didn't look like that would be happening any time soon.

If she was honest, she was a little wary of her dad. She didn't quite know what to say to him and it didn't feel very natural when he was around, though he'd never done anything to make her feel afraid. It was more about what wasn't there, what wasn't said, and a feeling that she wasn't really seen by him.

Sarah's feeling of uncertainty and dread about what was happening at home was quite confusing. It seemed like everything was coming to a head, but she had no idea what the outcome would be. Her mind wandered to the events of two days before, when she'd come home from school to find her mother sitting at the kitchen table, with her head resting on her hands, crying. She'd asked what was wrong, but her mother had just said: 'Nothing, I'm fine.' When she put her hand on her mother's shoulder, though, she'd started sobbing, with her shoulders heaving and tears falling into her hands. She'd impatiently tried to wipe them away, leaving trails of smudged mascara down her cheeks, pulling herself together, saying 'Really, I'm okay! I'd love a cup of tea'. Sarah, glad to have something to do, had gone to the cupboard and pulled out her mother's favourite mug — it had a turquoise, mosaic pattern on it and was really pretty. She boiled the water and tried to make it just the way she liked it, with a splash of milk, not too strong, and put it in front of her. Her mother had a sip and took a deep, shuddering breath. She'd then given her an uncertain look and eventually told her that she was afraid that her father was going to leave them. Her arms were crossed tightly across her chest, as if she was desperately trying to hold herself together, and her voice quavered as she spoke. Sarah suddenly felt incredibly vulnerable, just seeing her mother, an adult, trying not to fall apart. If her mother couldn't deal with this, what about her? She was just a kid.

She'd felt shocked at her mother's revelation — her stomach had clenched into a tight ball and she could feel her breathing so tight in her chest that for a moment she could hardly breathe. She'd felt sick and really scared, but at the same time must have been a bit numb, because she couldn't remember much about the next few hours until her father came home around six o'clock. She heard them having an argument, with raised voices, accusations and her mother sounding pleading, her father angry. She remembered moving to the door of the living room…

"I've tried and tried to tell you how unhappy I am, but it's always been all about you," her dad said. "I know you've been unwell, but you've let it blot out everything. We haven't done anything together for ages, and we don't even talk, other than bicker. I'm totally fed up with it and I need a break for a while."

It was the first Sarah had heard about her mother being unwell — she'd noticed that she'd been a bit withdrawn, but neither of them had said anything to her. That had been really confusing and made her stomach clench again. She felt sick. Her mother now sounded distraught.

"It's just so typical of you — when it gets hard, you just opt out! How can you leave us on our own? How will we manage? I bet you're having an affair with someone... Well, are you?" she demanded.

"I just don't know what to do any more. I've had it with trying to talk to you sensibly — I knew you'd try to throw it back at me. I'm going to check into a hotel for a while. Of course, I'll make sure you and Sarah are okay financially, I still love you both, but I can't go on like this and I really need to take a break. We both need a break if we're going to have any chance of working this out."

At that, Sarah had gone into the room and tried to persuade her dad to sit down at the table and eat dinner, summoning up all her powers of persuasion, trying to bring them together and make things better. She remembered standing between them, willing them just to do what she was asking them — she had the idea that if only he would eat with them, everything would be all right, but he walked straight past her, and out the front door. He'd taken nothing with him, just his car.

His departure had left a very long silence, heavy, like a grey blanket descending and sucking out the air. It was probably only for a couple of minutes, but it felt like it stretched on forever. She felt cold and shaky, but her mother didn't even make sure she was okay, she'd just left the room, walked along the corridor to her bedroom and closed the door. She heard her murmuring voice and presumed she was talking to someone on the phone. When she came out, she'd asked her to pack her pyjamas, a change of clothes and something to read, before taking her to her grandparents' house out in the countryside, twenty minutes away.

It was evening, and all that she could remember was staring back at the house as they left, with the street lamp shining on the bricks at the front, and a strange feeling that she was saying goodbye. Her mother had driven in silence, despite Sarah trying to find out what was happening — it was like talking to a wall. She'd dropped her off, looking very drawn and tired, and she hadn't spoken to her since. Sarah didn't know what was happening and wondered why no one would talk to her about it. Why did she feel that she was somehow responsible for making sure her parents were all right when they were the adults and didn't even seem aware of what it was like for her? She felt abandoned and was very grateful that she had her grandparents and their familiar house to be in.

Just thinking about it made her stomach tie itself in knots again, and to distract herself she looked at the wall across the room at a kind of plate hanging there that she'd always loved. Her gran had told her that it was something called a bas-relief sculpture — it looked very old and was of an old house, a mill beside a stream, and it stood out from the plate so that when she was day-dreaming it seemed almost real. Since she was really little, she'd imagined herself walking along the edge of the stream, dipping her bare toes into the water, climbing the steps and going into the house. As she stared at it now, she felt funny… Her eyes were drawn to the water-wheel, and she found herself noticing small details she'd never seen before — the water flowing in at the higher level of the river, pouring into the wheel, its slow turning — she couldn't look away. Her eyes slipped from the wheel to the edge of the river below and she could suddenly feel it cool on her feet, and was surprised to find her shoes and socks in her hand. She could hear the water bubbling over stones and could smell something like damp grass and maybe crushed lavender. Her foot slipped on a stone, but she shifted it to a dry one and managed to keep her balance. She then leapt to a patch of grass and climbed up the stony bank to the steps in front of the house — it seemed strange how often she'd done this before in her imagination, but never in a way that seemed so incredibly real. Maybe she'd fallen asleep and was dreaming? The stone of the steps was warm and smooth under her feet. They seemed well-worn and she counted seven of them to the flat platform at the top in front of the door. It was heavy and it creaked open; rays of sun hung on dust motes that made the inside look fuzzy.

Sarah walked into a living room that had a large, heavy wooden table, with four chairs arranged around it. One was pulled out as if someone had just walked away, leaving something that looked like a pottery beaker on the table. She looked across the room to a really big fireplace, with blackened tongs placed on the hearth in front of it, and some comfortable chairs clustered nearby. The room was dusty and felt neglected, as if someone had abandoned it unexpectedly, in a hurry, and hadn't returned.

Feeling a bit anxious about being in a stranger's house, she looked around and saw a corridor running straight ahead out of the room. Entering it cautiously, she could see that to her left, there was a large set of double wooden doors that were closed. Judging from the direction of the water-wheel, she imagined that the door would lead to work rooms for the mill. To her right, the door to the kitchen was ajar and she could see a thick, wooden bench, backed with blue and white tiles, and a set of stairs going upwards — presumably to the bedrooms. Although she was curious, she didn't explore, because the sun coming from the open door at the end of the corridor beckoned her.

Sarah had a strange sensation as she walked across the threshold at the doorway. For a moment, she felt dizzy and she put her hand out on the wooden frame to steady herself. *What on earth is happening — is this a dream or what? When am I going to wake up?* she wondered, as she walked down three worn, stone steps into the garden. It was a beautiful, sunny day and the garden, although overgrown, had obviously once been well planned. The path from the door led her through a border of lavender, behind which was a tangle of dark pink and white roses, both giving off a heady scent. Back further in the garden, she could see fruit trees growing amongst long grass and weeds. Bruised and bird-pecked plums, a deep bleeding purple, lay on the ground. The well-trodden path had small, smooth grey pebbles underfoot, and it took her towards the wooden gate and the field lying beyond.

She could see the river in the distance and her feet seemed to be strangely drawn towards it, looking much deeper and smoother than the water below the mill wheel had been. The bank on the other side sloped steeply down to the water, and had a stand of tall trees on its brow, their leaves shifting slightly in the light breeze, which seemed oddly warm and much nicer than the cold of her real world. She could hear birds calling from the trees, and the slow movement of water, with a distant bubbling sound as it moved over the stones below the wheel. The sun was hot on the back of her head and neck, and as she lazily batted a bee away from her face, she suddenly caught sight of a shape that gave off a yell and slid down the far bank, splashing into the water. She ran towards the river, her heart pounding.

Chapter II
When is Enough?

"Stop it! Stop making that dreadful noise, you know you deserved it! Go upstairs to your room and stay there until dinner."

Tom ran up the stairs and closed his bedroom door. He tried not to bang it, but it still closed more sharply than he meant it to. He held his breath, heart pounding, but nothing... He sank down to the floor beside his bed, back to the wall, with his arms tightly clasped around his knees, trying to control his sobs. When his heart stopped pounding so hard, he reached under his bed and pulled out a box, lifted the lid, and took out a worn bear. At twelve he was supposed to be too old for Brown Bear, but it didn't feel like that. He closed his eyes and crushed him to his chest, breathing in his familiar smell: of sun and sand and earth, of hugs and tears, and of fear, all meshed in his matted fur with a thousand memories.

When he opened his eyes again, Tom blinked away tears until he could see clearly. He found himself looking across the room at the old chest of drawers against the opposite wall. A large mirror was balanced on top, propped up against the wall. The mirror's wooden frame had a vine with leaves and tendrils intricately carved into it. It used to belong to his grandparents, then his dad — his grandfather did the carving, and he loved it. When he was upset, he liked to sit and watch it until he felt himself, small as an ant, clamber up inside the vine at the bottom left-hand corner. Higher and higher, hand over hand, the stem smooth and firm, hand and footholds where leaves sprouted out of its glossy surface, towards the top, where he would find his father's castle. His real father...

*

At dinner, Tom sat quietly, pushing his food around his plate with his knife. He wasn't hungry, even though the food looked nice enough. His throat felt constricted and he still had a lump of fear in his stomach. His mum sat opposite him, his sister beside him, and his stepfather, Gerald, was at the end of the table.

"Eat your dinner, Thomas," Gerald growled, rubbing his hand over the grey stubble on his chin, making a raspy noise. "You'll be staying there until you do!"

Nothing new, then. He had a routine — he counted to thirty and if no one had said anything to him before he got there, he would be able to swallow one small piece of food. If anyone said anything to him, he had to start counting over again. It meant he ate most of his food cold, but at least once everyone else got fed up waiting for him, he was left in peace. Twenty-six... twenty-seven... twenty-eight...

"Eat it!" yelled Gerald, scraping his chair back from the table as he stood up, and moving threateningly towards him. He wasn't very tall, but he was powerfully built, and the muscles of his tattooed arms rippled and twisted menacingly as he grabbed him by the hair at the back of his neck and pushed his head down towards his food. Tom quickly put a pea in his mouth, wondering how he would ever swallow since he hadn't got to thirty. He gagged, but it went down. Gerald waited until he put another one in his mouth, then strode off to the living room, slamming the door behind him. Tom sat, watching his mother. She looked pale and subdued and didn't seem to want to look at him, turning her gaze to the plates on the table, picking them up and moving past him to the kitchen, brushing his shoulder as she went past — he didn't know if she touched him on purpose or by accident.

Tom didn't usually lose it the way he had today. Normally, he managed to look kind of blank most of the time and not let anyone know how he felt, but today had been a bad one. He'd been caught trying to phone his grandparents — his dad's parents. His mum and Gerald had come home early, and even though he'd put the phone down straight away, Gerald dialled some numbers and the display showed him the last number that had been called. He wasn't allowed to talk to his grandparents. Once a year, just before Christmas, he and his sister saw them, but only with his mother and Gerald present, so he couldn't say anything to them. When he was ten, he'd rung and asked them to take him away to live with them. He'd spoken to his grandfather and could hear his grandmother crying in the background. They'd talked to each other while he was still on the phone, and he heard his grandmother saying something like they had to help or she (his mother maybe?) would kill him the same way she killed her husband. He didn't really understand that — his father died when he was only four — but it did scare him. Child Services came to see them soon after that, but his mum and Gerald were really nice to them and he couldn't really say anything with them around; he'd just hung his head and said he was all right. It was because of Child Services though that he got to see his grandparents at Christmas — there was some sort of agreement that had to be kept. He didn't know why Gerald and his mum disliked them so much. His mum didn't have any parents, and they were so nice.

Sometimes, when Gerald wasn't there, they did things like they used to, just small things like making pancakes together, but when he was around, she was unpredictable, sometimes subdued just doing what his stepfather said, but other times she was really scary and lashed out at him, or helped Gerald, like the time he tried to dodge out of his way around the table and his mum shifted the chair so Gerald could grab him more easily. That had led to a real thrashing. He didn't know what was worse, the pain and humiliation, or the betrayal of seeing his mother watching and not doing anything to help. His sister, Leah, didn't get into much trouble. She was three years older than him and just kept her head down and helped her mother in the kitchen as much as she could. She tried to look out for him, but was mostly too busy making sure she stayed out of trouble herself.

*

Saturday was hot but overcast. Chore day. Tom mowed the lawns and his sister did the housework while his mother and Gerald went shopping. The grass was long after a warm, wet week, which could be quite a challenge for the old, temperamental lawn mower. Tom wheeled it out of the garden shed, sighing with relief when it started on the second try. He began with the easy bit close to the garden where there weren't many bushes to manoeuvre around, just overgrown flowers with an edge he could mow close to. He then moved over to the grass in the middle, which was growing vigorously without any plants to suck up the rain. In the thickest part, the mower coughed and stopped. He started it again, but it only moved a few of his steps before stopping. *Damn!* He kept trying, getting hotter and more agitated each time. He kicked it, hurting his toe, with the only effect being more rust flaking off onto the grass. Eventually, he gave up and went into the house to cool down and get a glass of water, talking to Leah until she warned him it was close to the time his mum and Gerald would return. This time, the mower refused to even start. He flung himself down on the grass in frustration, wondering what he would do — excuses would be no good for Gerald. Just then, he heard the car drive up to the front of the house. A door slammed and he could hear raised voices. He jumped up and ran for the shed, shutting the door behind him.

The shed was small and piled up with gardening stuff; a bench with things like hedge-cutters and garden trowels; a broom and spade propped up in the corner against the wall; the floor strewn with dusty sacks of compost, packets of spray, sprayers, hoses... There was nowhere to hide so he crouched in the corner behind a tarpaulin and made himself as small as possible. If Gerald had come home angry, who better to take it out on than him? He heard him shouting in the garden, "Where are you, you little shit? Why haven't you finished the lawns?"

The door to the shed flew open, crashing against the wall. Heavy, angry footsteps came towards him and the next minute he was lifted by the back of his shirt and dumped on the tarpaulin. Tom caught sight of something swinging down towards him before turning his face protectively underneath him into the canvas.

*

Tom lay huddled on the tarpaulin, aware that every bone in his body felt pummelled and that he could taste something bitter in the back of his throat. He remembered throwing up at some point, whether at the pain of his beating, or in reaction to the hatred that poured out of his step-father, he wasn't sure. Feeling crushed and defeated, he wondered how he could pick himself up again and carry on; beyond even crying, just lying there staring at nothing, kind of numb somewhere deep inside. He heard the door handle turn softly and then quiet footsteps moving towards him. His insides clenched, but it was Leah, who crouched down beside him, pressing some coins into his hand and whispering, "Quick, you've got to get up, quietly. Go to the public phone on Hutchinson Street and ring Grandad. You've got to do it now while there's proof."

"Proof?"

"While you've got bruises, or else the same will happen as last time. I've got to go back, I just snuck out when he went upstairs." Her eyes flicked back in the direction of the back door of the house as a wave of anxiety spread through her. Tom pulled himself upright painfully as Leah opened the door and checked that the way was clear for her to return unseen.

"And, Tom... make sure he comes to get me as well... please!" She awkwardly patted him on the arm, hesitated, then ran quickly back to the house.

He stood up, feeling wobbly, as if all his bones had turned to jelly. Putting his head out the door, he couldn't see anyone in the garden but he could hear loud voices from upstairs — their room. Praying that they were too busy arguing to look out the window, he crept as quickly as he could along the side of the shed, around the corner, then quickly across to the hedge that ran along the side of the house. Safe from view, he ran to the front of the house and out the gate. Once outside, he ran and ran, heart pounding, down the road and, gasping for air, climbed over the stile that led to the park. Rather than running across the open ground where he might be seen, he zig-zagged through the trees and undergrowth that formed a wide belt along the edge. As he ran, he could feel low branches whipping against his bruises, and spiky weeds and thistles snagging his legs. He didn't stop, even though his legs felt like rubber. Running full pelt, he burst through a tangle of bushes and suddenly found himself sliding down a bank, slippery with old leaf mould. As he slid, he gathered speed and could see himself, almost as if in slow motion, as he plunged headlong into the shallows of the river at the bottom of the bank. Everything went blank.

Chapter III
In the Nick of Time

Sarah raced towards the water, stumbling over the uneven ground where trees had sent out spidery surface roots, erupting in peaks and fissures on its surface. She caught her foot on one of the roots and sprawled headlong onto the ground, grazing her palms and knees where she fell. She picked herself up, dusted off her hands and headed again for the river. She had to fight her way through long grass to get to the bank and as she burst through, she lost her footing and slid down the slippery bank to the water's edge. She could see a dark shape in the shallow water on the other side of the river. She wondered how deep it would be if she jumped into it — should she swim across? It was only about ten feet wide. But then, she saw that slightly downstream, before the watermill, large stones had been placed in the river to make a crossing. They looked like they'd been positioned there for adults and it was quite a leap between them, but she managed to get to the other side safely.

Sarah ran back upstream to where the lifeless form of a boy was lying face down in the water. He was about the same size as her, but when she tried to pull him out by grabbing his clothing, he felt so waterlogged and heavy that she didn't think she could do it. Eventually, she managed to half drag, half lift him to the stones on the edge of the river and pull him over onto his back. She thought he was still breathing but he didn't respond to her, and seemed to be unconscious. Remembering what she'd seen on TV, she dragged him onto his stomach, head turned to the side and pressed down on his back. A trickle of water came out of his mouth. He coughed and more water emerged. He coughed and spluttered again, and she turned him back onto his back. His eyes were open, green and bleary looking. He closed his eyes then re-opened them, focused on her and tried to sit up.

*

"Who are you…?" Thomas sat up, feeling wobbly and very disorientated. "Where am I?"

A girl around his age with fair hair and a worried expression on her face, was looking at him.

"I'm Sarah. That's the easy part. I don't know where we are — I thought I was dreaming, but here you are, much too real to be in a dream. Look at you — soaking wet and with a bump on your head!"

Thomas was puzzled. He shook his head a little — it hurt — he put his hand up to the back of his head and his fingers found a lump. "How did I get here? The last thing I remember was running through the trees…"

"Well, I saw you sliding down the bank — you yelled! When I got here you were face down in the water. See, you can probably feel where your head is grazed — you must have hit your head on a rock in the river," she said, with a look of concern on her face. She gently put a finger on his right temple, where little blisters of red were oozing out of his skin.

"But… it's the back of my head that hurts!" He was really

confused, partly because he really didn't understand what had happened, but also because his head felt so fuzzy. He began to try to get to his feet and Sarah put out her hand to help him. She pulled him up and he wobbled a little as he found himself upright. He felt dizzy and a bit nauseous — a headache was starting to spread from the back of his head with a dull, pulsing insistence.

"I guess we need to get you back up the bank so you can go home. Is it very far?"

"I'm not going back! I'll go anywhere, but not there."

"Oh! ... Can you make it over the crossing stones in the river to the other side then? I dropped my shoes and socks over there. Look, I'll take off my jumper for us both to hold onto in case you feel like you're going to slip."

"Why do you have a jumper? It's summer!"

"I don't know — it's all very confusing! How about we talk about it later when we find someone to take care of you?"

They made their way back over the river, with each of them holding an arm of the jumper, like a rope between them, Sarah leading the way. She half pulled him up the bank on the other side, grabbing onto the long grass for balance. Picking up her shoes and socks from the top of the bank, she started walking, barefoot, towards a line of trees she could see ahead, thinking there may be a road beyond. Thomas started off directly behind her, but with each step he felt more and more unwell. His feet started to drag and he felt as if he was going to lose his balance. Sarah looked behind and saw him struggling to keep up, so she dropped back and put out a hand to help him. He brushed her off, angrily pulling away from her.

"What's wrong? I was only trying to help."

"I don't want your help. Just keep walking."

Sarah, feeling miffed, continued walking, but not far from the trees she heard a thump and turned to see him crumpled in a heap on the ground. She ran over to him — his eyes were closed and his breathing was ragged. She put her hand on his shoulder but didn't get a response. She shook him; still no response. Feeling panicky, she looked around, but could only see the trees ahead and the field stretching out along the side of the river. Behind her was the empty mill house she'd just left. The only thing she could think to do was to go on and hope for some sign of people. Bending down, she carefully straightened him out and put her jumper under his head, noticing how pale and sickly he was looking. She then ran towards the trees.

Her intuition was right. As she made her way between the trees, she came to a road stretching out along them. It was a gravel road, tightly packed down, and obviously well used and cared for. There were no signs of any houses though, just endless fields and more trees. Feeling at a total loss, not knowing which way to walk, she sat down at the side of the road to think. She was scared — the boy didn't look at all well. She felt completely lost in a fantasy world that had all gone wrong. She was disoriented, didn't know the difference between reality and her imagination, and was suddenly responsible for a boy whose name she didn't even know. This suddenly seemed really important and she wondered why she hadn't thought to ask him what it was. As she sat there, biting her fingernails and worrying, she heard an approaching vehicle in the distance. Standing up, she could see a car moving quickly along the road towards her from her right.

Sarah stood in the middle of the road, waving her arms in the air. The car slowed down and pulled over, stopping several feet away. It looked unusual, kind of old fashioned, but it had moved almost silently. If it hadn't been for the cloud of dust following it on the unsealed road, she might not have noticed it approaching. It was covered in a thick layer of grime, but she could make out that beneath it the paint was a dark green. Through the windscreen she could see the head of a woman wearing dark glasses. The woman motioned impatiently to her to go around to the driver's window.

Sarah walked to the side of the car as the woman wound down her window, leaving her glasses on. She had long, reddish hair with streaks of grey, messily caught up at the back, with tendrils escaping snake-like down over her shoulders and back. She didn't say anything but had one eyebrow arched as if to say, 'So what's going on?' She was probably a bit older than her parents. Sarah found herself feeling flustered, as if she'd done something wrong and couldn't find her voice, until she remembered the boy lying back in the field.

"There's an injured boy lying behind those trees and I can't move him. Could you please help me? He needs to get to a hospital."

"An injured boy!" This was a statement rather than a question. "What's happened to him?"

"I don't really know. I found him unconscious in the river and pulled him out. He woke up, but when we were walking towards the road he collapsed and I couldn't get him any further," she said breathlessly.

The woman slowly removed her sunglasses and looked

Sarah up and down with deep hazel eyes that had unusual flecks of gold and green in them. Sarah felt squirmy and uncomfortable under her gaze.

"Well, I suppose I'd better take a look then." Taking her time, she opened the door and got out, gathering her skirt behind her. Her clothes were quite unusual; her mother would have called them 'hippy' clothes. They seemed to have been patched together from lots of fabrics into a tight top and a long, flowing skirt. Sarah strangely found herself liking it — it reminded her somehow of her grandmother's dress up box, filled with an odd assortment of clothes and pieces of fabric, and the magical jumble of colours and textures she used to create her imaginary games.

They walked together back through the trees and over the field to where the boy lay completely still on the ground. The woman bent down over him, putting her fingers to his wrist.
"His breathing and pulse are a little fast, but okay. What was he like before he collapsed?"

"He started off all right but got slower and stumbled a bit. He seemed quite grumpy, even though I was trying to help him!"

"It sounds like concussion — I see he has a bump on his head."

"He was complaining of one on the back of his head as well."

"I'm going to lift him and carry him to the car. Pick up the jumper and shoes and go ahead of me to open the back door."

Sarah went ahead as instructed, turning once to see the woman lifting the boy easily and draping him over her shoulder. *What?*

How did she do that? she thought in astonishment, opening the car door and placing her jumper down on the far end of the seat for his head to rest on. The woman brought him to the car and laid him along the back seat, telling Sarah to get into the front passenger seat.

"I'd rather sit in the back to make sure he's okay," she said, lifting his feet to climb in, and putting them down on her lap. "Can you please take us to the hospital?"

"Well, no, I can't. The city is a long way away and Hunterdale, the nearest town, doesn't have one. He only has concussion. I can take care of him — I'm a healer, and my place is only fifteen minutes from here. What's your name?"

"I'm Sarah — I don't know what his name is because I didn't get the chance to ask him."

The woman started the car and drove off in the same direction she'd been heading. Sarah sat in the back, tense and unable to relax, torn between wanting to be vigilant about where they were going and needing to keep an eye on the boy.

*

Shortly after, Tom started to wake up. He tried to sit up, but his head hurt and he felt really nauseous, with waves of feeling like he was going to throw up getting stronger every time he moved, so he put his head back down on Sarah's jumper. "What's happening? Where are we?"

"I found someone to help us. She's taking us to her house so she can make sure you're all right. You collapsed — she says you've got concussion from the bumps on your head and that her place is only about fifteen minutes away."

They were quiet for a while, Sarah noticing that the inside of the car was a bit like one she'd seen in a technology museum — something about the leather upholstery and burnished wood fittings. She was so confused by everything that she couldn't really take it in or think about what it meant. Tom interrupted her thoughts.

"My head's really sore. It's not just from falling into the water — I was running away from my stepfather — he hit me before I left."

"Oh! Has that happened before?"

"Yes, on and off when he gets into a rage. Never as bad as this time though — I really thought he was going to kill me!"

"That's terrible!" Sarah said, sounding shocked. "What about your mother? Didn't she try to stop him hitting you?"

Tom's eyes started to fill with tears, but he shut them and pretended he'd gone back to sleep.

A few minutes later, he opened his eyes again and said that if they were travelling about sixty kilometres per hour that meant her place was about fifteen kilometres from where he fell into the river.

"Do you always do that?

"Huh? What do you mean?"

"When you start to feel bad, turn it into thinking?"

"I don't know what you're talking about. And anyway, what's wrong with that?"

Sarah decided it wasn't a good idea to say any more — he obviously felt really bad about what had happened at home. "Kilometres? Where do you come from? I say miles."

"From Auckland?"

"Oh, Auckland, in New Zealand — my aunt lives there. I

thought you had a bit of a strange accent."

"So, where are you from?"

"Well, England of course."

"What do you mean 'of course'? Are you visiting your aunt?"

"No... I'm really not so sure of anything at the moment. I've been trying to work it out — I was at my grandparents' house and thought I went to sleep, but this doesn't seem much like a dream to me — you're much too real! And at home it's winter, and we don't have cars like this one. It seems like an old style but it's really quiet."

"Well, I don't know either. What can you see out the window?"

"Mostly just fields and trees, though I saw a cottage with some sheds a couple of minutes ago. Maybe it was a farm? I haven't seen any other cars. The road is quite smooth, but it isn't sealed. The trees and things seem similar to England, but it's definitely not winter!"

"It's summer in Auckland, but your description is nothing like it. I'm Thomas, Tom, by the way." Tom sounded matter-of-fact as they talked, but inside he was worried — about where he was, how he'd got there, and although he instinctively trusted Sarah, who was this strange woman who was driving them to her house?

The woman, Morwyn, was listening silently to their conversation, noting their bickering and trying to detect any irritations and tensions between them in case she could use them later. She was going to have to play out the next couple of days very carefully. She needed to give them enough time to create a bond, but not enough to build on any suspicions of her. She had to engage Sarah's need to care about Thomas, and the circumstances so that Thomas would think she'd abandoned him.

*

After driving for a little more than ten minutes, Morwyn took a left turn off the road, to a narrower lane that didn't look as well cared for. It had wheel ruts and potholes, and the car bumped and lurched, sliding a little on corners where the gravel was loose. Brambly looking hedges lined the road so that Sarah couldn't really see what lay beyond. The road led into some dense trees, with dappled light coming through the foliage, casting shimmering patterns on the road as the trees moved with the breeze. It would have been quite pretty if she hadn't felt so anxious. After driving for maybe a mile, the trees opened out to a small clearing. A stand of five trees stood in the middle of it, and to the side she could see a wooden building that might be a small shed, and some sort of raised vegetable garden.

As the car drew to a stop, Sarah wondered where the house was. This was clearly the destination, yet surely the shed wasn't where the woman lived?
"Where are we?"
"This is where I live. If you get out, I'll get Thomas when I'm ready. Thomas, stay lying down for a bit longer."
Sarah opened the door and got out of the car. The woman meanwhile had gone over to the stand of trees — they looked a bit like the tall oak trees in the park near her house, but with longer trunks. With the ones at home her dad had been able to

throw a swing over the lower branches for her, but he would never be able to do that with these ones. The woman was pulling on what looked like a chain running down the side of one of them, a bit like the action she made pulling up the French blind in her bedroom. She realised it was some sort of pulley and looked upward to see a wooden platform descending from between two of the trees. Looking beyond it, she could see a solid structure supported between the five trees and realised it could be the floor of a dwelling, suspended about three times the height of a house above the ground.

The wooden platform had reached the ground and the woman strode over to the car and lifted Thomas, again seemingly without effort, and placed him on the platform.

"Just lie there and don't move while I winch you up. We'll follow in a minute."

The platform was pulled up until its base was flush with the floor of the dwelling. The woman secured the pulley mechanism and then detached a rope fastened alongside it. Pulling on it unravelled a long rope ladder from the platform. It uncoiled itself and dropped down to the ground — two sturdy ropes, one either side supporting wooden rungs. She beckoned to Sarah and indicated that she should start climbing up the ladder. With some trepidation, Sarah began to climb. It was reasonably solid, though it drifted with her weight before the woman came over and held the end taut. She didn't look down, just focusing on each rung as she climbed higher and higher. Eventually, she got to the platform and managed to pull herself over the wooden edge. For a moment, she looked down and felt a wave of vertigo wash over her — they were up dizzyingly high. With a gulp and a deep breath, she turned and focused on Tom, still lying in the centre of the platform where he'd been left.

*

Tom was anxiously wondering about the last several hours as he lay waiting for whatever would happen next. From fleeing his stepfather's cruelty, then into this weird world of pain and fuzzy confusion, the intensity of Sarah and then to this woman who was helping them — it was all too overwhelming and confusing. Sarah seemed friendly and genuinely concerned about him, but she had a way about her that left him feeling exposed and vulnerable, as if she could somehow see the soft part of him no one (other than Brown Bear) had seen since he was little. The woman — well he'd been fascinated by the system of cogs used to raise the platform; it was really quite sophisticated, but why did she need to live so far above ground? And her car was a bit odd. Where were they? What was this land somewhere between, or parallel, to where he and Sarah had come from? Had he somehow willed himself here, far away from his family? He felt really scared and on edge. Home had been horrible, but at least it was known — everything here was out of kilter and he needed to make sense of it.

He realised that Sarah had made her way onto the platform, and raised himself onto one elbow as she came over to him. She was looking a bit pale and had a really tight expression on her face.

"I hate heights! Are you okay? You're looking a bit better."

"I'm all right, but I can't remember much since you pulled me out of the water — my head feels woozy."

"Well, that's not surprising given the knocks you've had to it, and that we're both somewhere very odd. I'm not at all sure about this place!"

Tom sat up and tried to get his bearings. The platform appeared to form part of a deck adjoining a dwelling that was probably the woman's house. It was made of broad planks of rough timber with a generous number of windows to let in the dappled light. Even so, he imagined it would be quite dark inside at times, being in the middle of trees. It had a double chimney — probably one for cooking and another for heating.

He'd just noticed the heavy wooden door with large locking bolts, when the woman appeared over the edge of the deck. She leaned over to the edge of the platform and appeared to lock something just out of their range of sight.

"Where are we?"

"At my house."

"But where is that? And how do we get home? We've both somehow ended up here from opposite sides of the world and we have no idea what's happened."

"It's good to see you sitting up — I heard you say that your name was Thomas." She turned to Sarah: "Why don't you help me to get him inside." She was clearly not about to answer his questions, and avoided eye contact with them. They both bent down and supported him either side to stand and walk, a little shakily, over to the door. The woman produced a large key from her pocket, unlocked the central lock and slid back the bolts. As she swung the door open, Tom vaguely wondered why the bolts were on the outside.

Inside was gloomy, as he'd imagined, but the woman quickly lit several lamps placed around the room, which gave it a welcoming glow. He could see that they were in a large living room shaped to lie within three of the five trees, so that there were two walls with windows facing out (including the one with the door and deck), and the other walls were internal. There were two skylights placed in the roof so that natural light was cast down onto large tables beneath each window. One of these was obviously where she did pottery. It was cluttered with implements for cutting and shaping clay, and an assortment of pottery in varying stages of completion. Some looked like containers, like bowls and cups, others seemed to be figurines — he couldn't make out any details from where he was standing. A pottery wheel was placed to the right of the table.

Looking around, the other table was piled with canvases, paints, brushes and an easel. From what he could see of it, her artwork was very dark and disturbing. Like, above the fireplace there was a huge canvas painted out in blacks, reds and greys in an abstract design that connected to something very disturbing and scary inside him. He quickly moved his glance away and noted the stacks of firewood beside the fireplace, the bookcases on the walls, and the floor that was cluttered with wooden boxes and pieces of furniture, including chairs, a small table and a large couch. Everything seemed to be made from wood, including the walls and floor. There were no curtains or blinds to soften the interior, and it would have been overpoweringly brown and dark if it wasn't for the lamps and splodges of colour on the book spines, and in the assortment of artwork.

Sarah was gazing around the room as well, looking quite overwhelmed. The woman had moved across the room and had opened one of the two internal doors that led into the kitchen. Sarah supported Tom to walk over to the couch, where he lay down, glad to be able to rest his fuzzy and aching head.

"How about we have a cup of tea first, then we'll take a look at Thomas's injuries?"

"That would be nice, thanks. Don't you have electricity then?"

"I don't need it. It's not easy to connect it this high up in the trees, so I decided to make do with the old ways."

"So why are you so high up?"

"Well, don't you think it's good to be different sometimes?"

"It's very private." Sarah actually wanted to say secluded, but thought that implied something sinister, which was in fact what her intuition was telling her. She shivered, feeling an icy creature walking down her spine, even though it wasn't cold.

Sarah could see the woman loading wood into some sort of large oven in the kitchen. Not long after, she lifted a heavy black kettle from the worktop, taking it to the bench. She scooped tea leaves out of a canister. Sarah glanced over at Tom — he was looking a lot better, with a bit of colour in his cheeks. The woman emerged from the kitchen carrying a tray holding three steaming pottery mugs of tea. Putting it down on a side table she arranged a large cushion behind Tom to prop him up and passed each of them a mug. It was hard to tell what colour it was in the dark mug, but it looked and smelt like herbal tea. It was piping hot and had a slightly bitter taste that she didn't like, so she put it back on the side table pretending to wait for it to cool.

"Do you mind me asking what your name is?" She hoped she wasn't being rude...

"I'm Morwyn. Welcome to my home."

Morwyn helped Tom to drink his tea and, when he'd finished it, eased him back into a lying position on the couch. A short time later, he drifted off to sleep, looking a little flushed but peaceful.

Morwyn beckoned Sarah over to the couch, where she gently examined the bump on his forehead.

"He told me he has one on the back of his head that really hurts."

"Yes, there's quite a big lump. He's been hit with a lot of force."

Morwyn was pulling up his T-shirt. He had mottled marks high up near his shoulders and on his upper arms.

"Help me to spread this cream on the bruises. I imagine he has more on his back, but I don't want to turn him until we get him onto the bed."

"What's the cream?"

"A mixture of herbs, but mostly witch-hazel and arnica for bruising. I grind the ingredients into a paste, then put them into a cream base that I get from the town."

They smeared the cream generously over Tom's arms and shoulders. He seemed deeply asleep and didn't even stir. Morwyn then went through the other internal door to a bedroom, returning soon after to lift Tom off the couch. Sarah followed her as she carried him through a bedroom that was obviously hers, to another room lying beyond. It was smaller and was an unusual shape, triangular — it was wedged in between the kitchen and Morwyn's bedroom, and all the rooms had to fit in around the five sides formed by the trees. It had room for a single bed, bedside table and small wardrobe. She placed him down on the bed and rolled him away from them onto his left side. Pulling up his shirt they could see angry welts across his back and shoulders.

"They're going to turn into very nasty bruises, though the arnica will reduce the swelling and help them to fade."

After covering them in cream, Morwyn eased him onto his back and pulled a light cover over him.

"I'm afraid you'll have to sleep on the couch. This is the only spare bed."

"That's okay, it looks comfortable. Thank you for helping us. How long do you think it will take him to get better?"

"I don't know. Concussion can affect people differently, depending on how hard they've been hit and where. You can stay here as long as you need."

Back in the living room Morwyn invited her to finish her tea, but Sarah said she wasn't thirsty at the moment. She was wondering what to say to her and how they'd spend the time while Tom was asleep, but Morwyn soon announced that she had to go out for a while to do some errands and may not return until after she was asleep. She showed her where she could find some bread, cheese and apples in the kitchen and then left, using the rope ladder once again. It was with some relief that Sarah heard her start the car and drive away. She needed time to think about all that had happened and what it meant.

First, she decided to properly explore the house. The living area was much as it appeared — a mixture of work areas, relaxation and storage, and was probably the place Morwyn spent most of her time. The books looked well used, and were mostly fiction and botanical works, though there were several encyclopaedias and books of myths and legends. Up high, out of her reach, there were older volumes with symbols on the spines that she didn't recognise. The canvases on the table and stacked between the table and the wall, were mostly dark and abstract, although there was a pile of very well drawn watercolour paintings of herbs that she liked. They looked as if they could be used as illustrations in a plant book.

She looked out the windows and could only see the trees, and far below, a corner of the vegetable garden and shed. When she went over to open the door to let in more light, she found that it was locked. She felt a bit worried, but brushed it away, thinking that Morwyn must have locked it to make sure they stayed safe in her absence. Anyway, she didn't much fancy the possibility of sleep-walking off the edge of the deck!

The kitchen was a triangular shape, with the oven, a clay-tiled bench and sink on the outer wall with a window above, and the internal wall without the door (the other side of the inner wall of Tom's room) lined with cupboards and shelves. The cupboards mostly held food supplies, plates, mugs, containers and cooking equipment. One of them was locked. On the shelves beside the cupboards were rows of neatly arranged jars. They were all labelled and looked extremely well organised by size and contents. Some were filled with herbs, both leafy and ground, others contained liquids sorted by colour — deep reds, browns and yellows. It looked a bit like an old-fashioned pharmacy — she thought she remembered they used to be called apothecaries. There was a large mortar and pestle made of stone on the bench that was obviously used for grinding the herbs into powders. It was a bit like an overgrown version of the one her mother used to grind up herbs and spices for curries. The writing on the labels was mostly in a language she didn't understand. She thought it might be Latin, because she recognised some of the names of the herbs like *chamomilla recutita* and *cinnamomum verum* — they must be chamomile and cinnamon. She saw one that said *digitalis* and frowned. She remembered her grandfather taking her for a walk near the woods when she was young, and getting upset with her when she picked some pretty pink and purple flowers and put them upside-down on her fingers. He'd told her they were poisonous and never to put them near her mouth, making her wash her hands. They were called foxgloves and when she'd told him that was much too nice a name for a bad plant, he'd told her its real name was *digitalis*. Why would Morwyn keep that in her kitchen? Why was one of the cupboards locked?

Next, she made her way to Morwyn's room. It was cosy. She had a double bed with a wooden headboard and a patchwork quilt in autumn colours thrown over it. There was a rug on the floor in similar colours — the light shining on it through the window above the bed made the room look warm and comfortable. A wicker chair stood in one of the corners beside a small table with a book and a clock on it. She realised it was already six o'clock — she'd completely lost all her sense of time since plunging into this strange world. A door in the outside wall led to a tiny bathroom built around the exterior side of one of the trees. It had a basin and mirror, a shower that didn't even have a curtain, just a grill in the floor for the water to drain into, and a wooden box with a seat on it that must be the toilet. Back in the bedroom the only other piece of furniture was a wardrobe, quite large, made of dark wood. It looked a bit like the old-fashioned one in 'The Lion, The Witch and The Wardrobe'. She gingerly opened the door, feeling bad about prying, and saw a multitude of dresses hanging there, all quite dark and long, many made of fabric that looked like the patchwork one she'd been wearing that day. There were a couple of jackets and several pairs of shoes at the base of the wardrobe, also dark — either black or brown leather. Two drawers sat at the base of the wardrobe, containing underwear and cardigans.

Sarah then checked on Tom. He was sleeping deeply, lying on his back with his mouth slightly open. She quietly left his room and returned to the kitchen where she cut herself a couple of thick chunks of bread, making a sandwich with a slice off the slab of tasty cheese Morwyn had left out for her. Feeling a bit more settled, she lay down on the couch, pulling the blanket up to her chin. She had so much going on in her head. Thoughts about where she was, whether her grandparents were worrying about her, a bit of her secretly pleased her parents would have to think about her for once instead of themselves. What was wrong with her mum? A few months ago, she hadn't seemed well — she was pale and tired. Once she'd heard her retching in the bathroom. A couple of days later there had been a bit of a flurry about something, and her father got her to go to her friend's after school. He'd picked her up after dinner and when they got home her mum was in bed, where she'd stayed for a couple of days. They just said she was 'feeling under the weather'. Since then, she'd been a bit depressed and moody, but she hadn't thought much about it. She also thought about Morwyn. She seemed nice and had been really helpful, so why was she feeling prickly and uncomfortable about where they were? She didn't think she would sleep, but before long she drifted off.

*

"Sarah, Sarah." Tom shook her shoulder. He'd woken from a deep sleep with a really woozy head. It felt like he was coming back to his body from down a long tunnel. He got out of bed and stumbled in the pale light from the moon, through Morwyn's empty bedroom to the living room, and saw Sarah curled up on the couch, her fair hair rumpled around her face on the cushion. He shook her shoulder, then did it again a little more firmly. She stirred, then all at once woke and sat up in one move.

"Oh, you gave me a fright!" Her heart was thumping and the hairs on her arms were standing on edge. "What time is it? Is Morwyn back yet?"

"Her room is empty. Where did she go?"

"I'm not sure; she left in the early evening saying she had errands to do. How are you feeling?"

"Quite a bit better, though my head's still sore. I've been puzzling over where on earth we are, though, and how I got here — that just makes it hurt more! Is there anything to eat?"

"Yes, I'll make you a sandwich while you look around.

She seems to have locked the door, so I'm guessing she's gone for the night."

Tom checked out the house while Sarah was in the kitchen. He was looking out one of the windows when she returned to the living room.

"This window opens, but the one over the deck doesn't. Makes it impossible to get out of here, because other than on the deck side, there's only a small ledge all the way around the rest of the platform, almost wide enough to inch around, except that the planks the walls are made of are so tightly wedged together that there are no handholds. We can't climb down one of the trees because they've had the branches below the platform taken off, and they're too high to slide down."

Sarah walked over to stand beside him looking down at the ground below. "It sounds as if Morwyn has something to hide, or built it expecting to need to keep something in! I'm getting a bit freaked about all of this — I'm glad you're feeling better — I wouldn't like to be working out what's happening on my own!"

They walked back over to the couch so Tom could eat his sandwich. He suddenly said, "Hey, I've lost track of time a bit, but I'm thinking today might be my birthday."

"That's weird — if it's the 8th of February, then it's mine as well — I'll be thirteen."

"Me too! That's really freaky!"

There was a long pause. Sarah suddenly felt overwhelmed — her brain had turned to mush and she couldn't get it to think about what was happening. It was as if they were part of something much bigger than them, as if they were pawns in some sort of game they didn't yet know how to play. Tom broke the silence. "Wow, that's a massive coincidence. I wonder what our families are thinking without us there. They must be wondering where we are by now. Anyway, happy birthday."

Sarah suddenly felt tears welling up. "Happy birthday to you too… I hope they miss me. Everything's so weird — what if we just don't exist at home any more?"

"Wouldn't bother me if I never saw them again, though I wouldn't want to upset my grandparents — if anyone ever told them I was missing!"

They broke off their conversation as they became aware of a tapping noise. It was rhythmic and seemed to be coming from the window Tom had been looking out. He went over, but couldn't immediately see anything. He then looked down and could see something grey and furry reaching up to tap on the lower portion of the window. He opened it and, in an instant, something jumped up onto the windowsill and then down onto the floor of the living room.

Chapter IV
"I believe cats are spirits, come to earth"
(Jules Verne)

"Oh, aren't you gorgeous!" Sarah ran her hand down the cat's silky fur. The cat arched her back under Sarah's hand and rubbed around her legs. Sarah caught sight of a slightly disconcerted look on Tom's face and said, "You don't need to be scared of her. Look, she likes you!" The cat had delicately raised one front paw and touched it to Tom's leg, before placing it back neatly beside the other on the floor. "See, she's being careful not to scare you!"

"How do you know it's a she?"

"Oh, I don't know, I can just tell — look at her — she has a feminine energy."

For an instant, Tom thought he got what she meant, then the perception disappeared, leaving him feeling grumpy that she knew something that he didn't. "I've never had a cat. I don't really know what to do with them."

"It's more like what she'll do with you. She'll let you know exactly what she wants. I wonder what she's doing here — she can't possibly belong to Morwyn — they don't go together."

"Now, I don't know what you're talking about again!" Tom grumbled. "I don't get why you're interested in a cat anyway when we don't know where we are or how we got here."

The cat followed them over to the couch and jumped up, curling into the space between them. Tom tentatively stretched out his hand and rubbed her head. Then, when she didn't object, moved his hand down her back, watching the way her luxurious grey coat rippled under his touch. She broke into a purr and he felt an odd sensation well up inside him, making him want to smile.

"Rub your hand under her chin and see what she does."

He stroked the white patch under her chin with one finger and marvelled as she stretched out her neck and leaned into his hand. He felt strangely happy and realised he'd never experienced anything responding to him in such a simple, affectionate way. It really was as if she liked him.

"What will we call her?"

He instantly knew what to say. "How about Hermione? She's my favourite character in Harry Potter."

"Yeah, I like that. And I'm sure she's going to be a little magical — cats always know so much more than we think!"

They were sitting together in companionable silence, with so much they could be wondering and worrying about, yet without any immediate need to do so, when they heard the sound of an approaching vehicle. Quick as a flash, Hermione ran across the room, jumped to the windowsill and out to the ledge beyond. They noticed that it was dawn — they could hear birds in the trees and could see through the skylights that the sky was starting to streak with morning light, mottled with a few slow-moving clouds. Then they heard the sound of the winch and realised that Morwyn was lowering the platform. It was raised again and, soon after, they heard the bolts in the door being scraped back and the key turn in the lock. They glanced at each other. Sarah had an unaccountable feeling of anxiety in her stomach and chewed nervously on the corner of her bottom lip, while Tom felt like he'd been abruptly woken out of a pleasant reverie and had a bemused look on his face.

Morwyn came into the living room with a box of provisions and two bags of clothes. She made no comment about where she'd been, but gave them the clothes and prepared them some eggs and a cup of tea for breakfast. They looked through the clothes: a couple of cotton tops for each of them, shorts and some long pants for Tom, and a skirt and more leggings for Sarah. Tom decided to change his clothes right away since they were muddy from his slide down the bank. He came out in the pants and a shirt and Sarah burst out laughing; the baggy grey pants were quite unlike anything he might have worn before, hanging about his ankles like a Shar-pei dog with too much skin. He looked offended, and Sarah wondered why he seemed to be so huffy, but he then looked down at himself and managed a wry smile.

Not long after, Tom started yawning and said he was still really tired and needed to go back to bed for a while. Morwyn was occupied with putting things away in the kitchen, so Sarah picked up a book and curled up on the couch to read, drifting off to sleep herself. She woke a couple of hours later to find Morwyn coming out of her room, looking concerned.

"I'm worried about Thomas. He seems to have relapsed. I've tried all the healing options I have and he's not improving. It's partly his concussion, but now I'm thinking that it's more than that, that somehow the darkness he was trying to escape has taken hold of him like a deep malaise, an illness of the mind as well as the body. When people have gone through the sort of trauma he has, sometimes a part of them closes down and they just don't want to be here anymore," she said, looking very serious as she stopped near her on her way to the kitchen.

"Oh, no! But he was so much better last night. He was talking and laughing as if he was completely recovered." Sarah started to feel panicky. Even though she didn't feel comfortable with Morwyn, at least she'd thought that because she was a healer Tom was going to be okay.

"Yes, it can be quite confusing. Concussion can come and go. I suggest we just keep an eye on him for the next twenty-four hours. Hopefully, he'll bounce back like he did last night."

For the rest of the day, Morwyn kept Sarah occupied by getting her to help around the house. She weeded the vegetable garden, picked the ripe vegetables and cut them up in preparation for dinner. In between, she checked on Tom. His colour didn't look good. His skin was pale and pasty looking, but at the same time he was sweating and his pulse was racing. She put a cool cloth on his forehead and sponged down his arms and chest. He was restless and she could see his eyes flickering under his eyelids. She mentioned to Morwyn that he seemed quite agitated and wondered if that was normal for concussion. Morwyn brushed off her concerns and didn't seem to want to talk about him, but at the same time became increasingly watchful of him. She spooned water into his mouth every few hours to keep him hydrated.

At one point, when Sarah was on her own with Tom, she was thirsty and went to take a sip of the water from his mug and found that it had a musty smell that put her off. She put her finger in it and licked it — it was bitter like the tea they'd been given the first evening, so she didn't have any. When she mentioned it to Morwyn, she just said to stop being picky — that the water was sometimes brackish by the time it was pumped up to the treehouse.

That night, when Morwyn had left again for wherever it was she went at night, Sarah heard Hermione tapping on the window as she was moving from Tom's room to the living room in search of more water. She let her in and picked her up and gave her a hug, loving the feeling of comfort it gave her to stroke her soft fur.

"It's so good to see you, Hermione. I've been wondering what on earth is wrong with Tom. He's so unwell, I don't know what to do about him — he's much worse than when we arrived here."

"You have good intuition — you need to trust it!"

Wow, such a clear voice in her mind. She looked around in surprise, trying to figure out where the voice was coming from. She thought it was a bit like those dreams she had when the wise woman who sometimes appeared, talked to her... She put Hermione down on the floor.

"He doesn't look good. Don't trust Morwyn."

What? The voice was so clear it was as if someone was talking to her, but the only living thing she could see was Hermione, looking at her with a slightly disdainful look in her green eyes.

"Was that you?" Hermione just raised her left paw and

daintily licked it before placing it back on the ground. "If that was you, say something else... please!"

"You mean 'think something' don't you?"

"That's amazing! How do you do that?" She picked her up and gave her another hug. Hermione lightly kneaded her shoulder with her front paws and purred.

"I wonder whether she's giving him something to keep him asleep," Sarah wondered.

"Yes, she knows about herbs — she could easily be giving him a sleeping draught."

The more Hermione 'spoke' the easier Sarah found it to understand her. It was like tuning into a radio station and gradually fiddling with the dial until it became clear. She stayed a while longer before disappearing out the window again with the assurance that she'd come back tomorrow. Sarah tried to find out where she went to, but only got a haughty, "Around about!"

*

The next day, Morwyn called her to Tom's room.

"Sarah, he isn't improving at all. If anything, he's slipping further away. I'm wondering whether he's giving up the fight to stay here."

"But what can we do? There must be something." Sarah felt sick with worry. "Can you take him to the hospital?"

"No, it's too late for that. It's far away and I'm afraid he probably wouldn't last the journey. I've been wracking my brain for something and I can think of just one possibility, although it's a long shot."

"What is it? We have to try anything we can."

"Well, we've had a tale passed on to us over the years. It's written in one of my books and I think it could well be true, but it's a bit complicated... There's a healing elixir that's said to exist in a very rare honey found in the mountains south of here. It's supposed to be a true story, but I don't personally know anyone who's managed to find it, although several have tried. The problem is that I can't go looking for it myself. Apparently, the path up the mountains is narrow and crumbling in places and won't take the weight of an adult."

"So I could get it!" It seemed the obvious answer to Sarah, without thinking through what that might mean.

"It's not quite that simple. There are a number of steps you would have to take to make sure you could get it safely, and even then, it would be very challenging for you. I wouldn't want you to come to any harm, and I'm not sure I should even be telling you about it."

Sarah felt very dubious about this — Morwyn didn't seem the sort of person to be worried about harm coming to her, especially if it was possible that she was trying to drug Tom. It was more likely that she was trying to trick her, so she decided to reply as if she believed her.

"I might look small, but I can be very stubborn and determined when I'm doing something for someone I care about."

"So, how about I tell you what's involved and you can make up your mind when you know more. Come over to the table and sit down. I'll get the book. It describes what you would need to do to find the honey, if that's something you're really willing to do."

Morwyn sounded so reasonable, but Sarah knew she had to keep her wits about her as she moved from the couch and sat on one side of the table as Morwyn pulled a dusty and old-looking book from one of her bookshelves and began her explanation. "On Greyvyn Mountain, which is actually a volcano, quite high up, there grows a very rare form of blue narcissus flower. Bees take the nectar, and the honey they make from it has what is said to be magical healing properties. The only way the guardian of the honey will allow you to have any is if you take two things with you. He requires a piece of gold thread as payment, and will only allow you to take as much honey as will fit into a small, special golden container, not a drop more. If anyone was foolish enough to try to take it without meeting his terms, the hive would turn on them. The bees are large and vicious, and stings from a swarm of them causes death."

"So, where do I find the thread and container?" Sarah said, trying to speak bravely, even though she was scared. "Do you have them?"

"That's part of the problem. I'll show you a map and explain it to you."

Morwyn went back to the book shelves and rummaged through some rolled up papers, eventually finding the one she wanted. She spread out a map hand-drawn in black ink on the table, putting their mugs on the top corners to hold it open. The map was titled 'North Feasgar'.

"So, is that the name of this land then?"

"Yes. Here in the west, you can see the road where I picked you up, just about here." She pointed to a spot, near which Sarah could see the river, labelled the Willis River, and a place called Riverstone, which would be the mill. The road headed north east, then curved over to the east to a town called Hunterdale. Morwyn pointed to where the treehouse was located about half way between Riverstone and the town.

"You would need to make your way to the town first, to Hunterdale. That's where the thread and container are."

"How would I get there?"

"I could get you a bike that you could use." She pointed to a mountain in the south. "The quickest way from Hunterdale to the mountain is to go down the river to Greyvyn village by boat. I can give you money for the river boat — it goes down river at nine in the morning and one in the afternoon, returning at midday and four in the afternoon."

"What's the river like?"

"Quite swift in places, but not too rough. You could go in a canoe if you're experienced, but the boat is safer. Obviously, it would be much easier for you if I drove you, but I'm afraid to leave Thomas in case his condition gets worse. He's not fit to travel with us."

"What's this in the middle of the map?" asked Sarah, frowning.

"It's a labyrinth. No one knows when it was built — it's very old. It's not somewhere you need to worry about — you don't need to go there and it's said to be dangerous."

"I thought labyrinths were meant to be peaceful places. There are quite a few where I come from. My mum says that walking them gives you a feeling of timelessness and peace. My grandparents have visited lots of them."

"Well not this one. I don't know anyone who's gone there and returned. Now, I need to talk to you about the tasks."

Morwyn then described how to find her friend, Dervla's, house in the town. She said Sarah should tell her that she was there to call in the favour she owed Morwyn — Dervla would know what that meant. Sarah was to ask for a golden thread, a bed for the night, and to be able to leave the bike there until she returned for it. She then told her that a man called Willard had the container and that she'd need to steal it from him — he wouldn't be willing to give, or even sell, it to her. Sarah stared at her aghast.

"I can't just go into his house and steal it!"

"Well," Morwyn did the raised eyebrow thing Sarah had noticed before and shrugged, "If you don't want to help Tom... It's not as if Willard is a good man!" and walked off towards the kitchen. If Sarah could see Morwyn's face she knew it would be oozing disdain, and she felt conflicted. She knew it was wrong to steal, and yet at the same time, was she just wimping out because she was scared, or because she'd been taught to be 'good'? If Sarah didn't do it, how would she and Tom ever get away from Morwyn? Her head said she shouldn't, but her heart said she should. Was she just putting rules ahead of things that were more important really? She thought about her family. *Dad would say I shouldn't ever steal, but mum would say sometimes rules have to be broken, if it's for the greater good. So would my grandparents.* It was so complicated and confusing. Sarah walked slowly to the kitchen and addressed Morwyn's back.

"I'm sorry, Morwyn. Please keep telling me about the tasks."

Morwyn turned towards her with a slight smile still lingering around her mouth, and Sarah wondered again about having to do what Morwyn wanted, when clearly, she wasn't to be trusted. Morwyn's expression was smug, knowing that Sarah would give in, and that she'd won!

Morwyn explained where to find Willard's house, adding that he went to the town market on three days of the week, including tomorrow, so she was to wait until nine in the morning to go to his house after he'd left. He kept a spare key on the lintel above the door in the garden shed behind the house. She was to go into the house, find his bedroom and take a wooden box from the dresser. The golden container, a small casket, would be locked inside it — she'd have to use her ingenuity to get it out, even it if meant smashing the box.

"So why can't I just ask Willard for the container?"

"Oh no, you won't be doing that, not if you want to get away with your life. Willard wants the elixir for his own selfish needs and wouldn't care that someone else may need it more."

"So, how do you know it's there?" Sarah asked.

"Never mind about that. I just do," she snapped.

Dismissing Sarah's worries, she outlined how she would need to get to the riverboat by midday, avoiding being seen by Willard, especially if he returned from the market and noticed that the box was missing. As Morwyn spoke, she was tapping her fingers unconsciously on the map. The noise started to get under Sarah's skin, adding to her increasing sense of anxiety. There were so many loose ends where things could go wrong. Any one of them could mean she failed. And somewhere during the conversation it had shifted from what she *could* do, to what she *would* do. How had that happened? She bit down hard on the corner of one of her fingernails and yelped with pain. It was a horrible habit she had when she got really worried. She stood up and started pacing around the room to give her agitated body something to do, until Morwyn resumed her instructions.

"When you get to the village, you then need to make your way just beyond it to the beginning of a track that curls round the side of the mountain as it starts to get steeper. This is the dangerous bit for me — it's very narrow in places, and there is little to hold onto and a big drop on one side. Just focus on looking ahead, one foot at a time. When you get about half way up, when you're approaching the tree line, the path gets easier and you'll begin to see small blue flowers growing on the side of the path amongst the vegetation."

"What's the tree line?"

"It's the point where the trees stop growing because it gets too cold for them. You'll be going up quite high and once you get beyond the tree line, not much grows except tussock — the old volcanic rock beneath won't support any other plant life. According to the book, when you see the blue flowers, you'll have gone slightly too far and you need to turn to your right, walk fifty paces, then face downhill and walk down another fifty paces to where you'll find a small wooden hut in a stand of trees. One of them is almost bare of leaves and you'll see the beehive hanging between two branches, close to the trunk." Morwyn broke off for a minute to take a sip out of the mug she had beside her on the table. "Then, the book says you take the thread and container to the beekeeper. He's supposed to be one of the last of the Little People and it says that he spends his days weaving, and uses the golden thread to weave into the fabric he makes, though no one knows what he does with it. If he accepts your payment, he'll fill the container for you and you can leave with it. The legend says that the bees are large, so you won't want to make them angry. In case they get nasty, I'll give you a potion to put on to stop them stinging you. You then just need to make your way back on the boat to Hunterdale, pick up your bike and return here. So that's all there is to it. What do you think? Is it something you can do?"

All there is to it? Sarah thought to herself. *A bit of an understatement!* She was aware that Morwyn was trying to manipulate her to get the elixir, and if she was drugging Tom, it wasn't really about saving him. What did she want it for? She'd have to hope for a chance to talk to Hermione to find out what to do. To buy herself some time, she pretended to go along with it and said that she was willing to do it for Tom.

"Good. I'm going to go now to borrow a bike from a neighbour." Sarah thought Morwyn had a strange look on her face as she spoke; calculating and smug maybe. When she noticed Sarah looking closely at her, she switched on a smile that didn't reach her eyes and rushed to get away. "No time to be lost — you'll want to be at Willard's in time for market day tomorrow. I'll be back in about an hour. You'll need to get going so that you have plenty of time to get to the town and to Dervla's before evening. It's a little further than our drive from the mill to here, so it may take you a while."

When Morwyn left, Sarah sat down on the couch, realising how scared she was feeling. She started churning through all the things she had to remember to do, and it seemed overwhelming. What would happen if Willard caught her? What if she couldn't get up the mountain? What if the bees wouldn't let her take the honey? What on earth was she doing in this place? A feeling of panic started to take hold of her and her chest felt tight. Her breathing came in short gasps as if it was being strangled in her chest and throat. Her throat knotted up so tightly she could hardly swallow and she started to feel dizzy. She tried to breathe more deeply, but her mind kept going back over and over the details of what she had to do. A small part of her mind knew that she just needed to do it step by step, but overwhelm stole that part away and she became totally locked into worry. She wrapped her arms around her chest and rocked where she was sitting, telling herself over and over that she couldn't do it, she didn't have to do it, she could run away. Slowly though, as she exhausted her trapped thinking, she started to remember what her father said about the way she and her mother got overwhelmed. He said that they 'negatively anticipated' and what was the point of wasting so much time worrying about something that might never happen? She tried again to breathe deeply and began to calm down.

She found herself still sitting on the couch with her arms locked around herself as if she was giving herself a hug, and realised that for ages her eyes had been unconsciously focusing on a symbol on the spine of another book sitting on the table. The cover was made of burgundy leather with beautiful golden lettering on it. She went over to the table and saw that it had symbols on the front cover as well — maybe they were runes or something; they looked a bit magical. The title on the front said 'A Book of Ancient Languages'. She opened it and the cover page had the same pattern as the one on the spine.

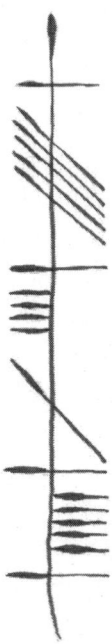

Underneath it had the title 'Anam Cara'. She flipped to the index at the back. Page 36… Sure enough, there it was, with a description that said:

'A person to whom you can reveal the hidden intimacies of your life. This friendship is an act of recognition and belonging. When you have an Anam Cara, your friendship cuts across all convention and categories. You are joined in an ancient and eternal union with the friend of your soul… and with humanity, in a way that cuts across all barriers of time, convention, philosophy and definition. When you are blessed with an Anam Cara, you have arrived at that most sacred place: Home.'[1]

She liked that. She really liked the idea of having a soul friend. Maybe that's what Tom was meant to be to her — there seemed to be something at work that had thrown them together and she couldn't let him down now. Sarah was distracted from her thoughts by a scratching at the window behind her, and realising it would be Hermione she turned to let her in. She picked her up, burying her face in her fur, breathing in her cat smell and, more importantly, her calm and wisdom.

"You have no idea how much I need your advice right now. I'm worrying about Morwyn — she feels 'wrong' somehow. Even when she's talking in a completely reasonable way, my intuition tells me that she's wearing a mask and if it slips, she'll be an evil witch person. And what's even worse, is that somehow, I keep finding myself wanting to do what she wants. Why do I always try to be 'good' when people want me to do things? And why would Morwyn have such bad inside her, or am I just imagining it? My dad always says my imagination is too vivid."

"Maybe both of you are afraid inside but it comes out in different ways. You try to make things better, smooth things over, even when you need to say no to something; and perhaps terrible things have happened to her that have pushed her in the other direction. Fear that can't be managed causes people to do terrible things, either to themselves or to others." Hermione licked her on the hand reassuringly.

"So, what do I do now?"

"You know you need to go. I'll look after the boy. You need to put me down now; we don't have much time to talk." With that, she leapt out of Sarah's arms and started pacing up and down the room, swishing her tail. "Tell me what Morwyn has said you need to do."

Sarah told Hermione what she knew of her tasks. Hermione had quite a lot to add — Morwyn knew about the box because she'd been seeing Willard for some time. Hermione also knew a bit about the tense relationship between Dervla and Morwyn. On the surface they were friends, but Dervla had tried to steal Willard off Morwyn. It hadn't worked, but Morwyn had felt betrayed and angry, and Dervla now owed her to try to make up for it. Morwyn's relationship with Willard was even more complicated.

"They're known to be lovers — that's where she goes most nights, but they both want the elixir desperately and will betray each other to get it, because they can only take enough for one," Hermione said. "The elixir is supposed to delay the aging process. Morwyn has used herbal remedies for years to keep herself young and extra strong, but they no longer have the power to ward off her physical decline. She knows about the casket, so it seems odd that Willard either trusts her not to take it, or is arrogant enough to think he can better her. He won't know that Morwyn's sending you though, so that'll give you an advantage. Meanwhile, there are rumours that he's making something to take him up the mountain, given that he's too heavy to attempt the climb himself."

They sat together for a while, quietly thinking about what lay ahead, Sarah calming herself by stroking Hermione's fur.

"So, can I 'think' to you as well, or do I have to speak?"

"Why don't you try and see?" Hermione replied.

Sarah tried first of all sending her a thought-picture of Tom lying on his bed asleep.

"Yes, he is very unwell, in his body and soul. But it's

being made worse by Morwyn. She's giving him the sleeping draught to make sure he can't talk to you before you leave. If he thinks you've left him, she'll be able to manipulate him more effectively."

"But can't you tell him why I've gone?" This time she tried thinking in words.

"He can't hear me yet — that may come later. In the meantime though, if you write a message, I can make sure he gets it."

"Your journey is going to be difficult," Hermione continued while Sarah wrote a note for Tom. "Be sure to stay calm, be brave and stick to your tasks. If you can do that, you'll get help when you most need it. Take some of the sleeping draught Morwyn has been using for Tom. Gossips say that Willard drinks a lot — you may need to lace his beer to get the golden casket. You'll find the draught in the kitchen in a jar labelled '*Atropa Belladonna*'. Don't use too much or you'll kill him — Morwyn has a measure with a mark on it for Tom, so double it for a grownup. You can take one of the containers from the cupboards."

Sarah went to the kitchen and carefully measured *Belladonna* into a small container, then on impulse doubled it, thinking it was better to be safe than sorry. As she walked back to the living room, she saw Hermione jump onto the windowsill. She sent her a message of courage and warmth as she disappeared over the side. An instant later, she heard the rattle of the ladder that heralded Morwyn's return. Morwyn was eager to send her on her way, but Sarah first went to see Tom. He was still lying in a fitful sleep — she smoothed a lock of dark hair away from his damp forehead and felt a sense of protectiveness and emotion welling up in her. She'd only met him for the first time the day before, but there was something about him, about where they were, and how they'd got here that made it feel much longer. He was her only link back to where they'd come from. Her eyes started to tear, but she brushed them away, wanting to make sure she didn't show any signs of weakness in front of Morwyn.

Sarah was given the potion to ward off bee stings, the map, money for the boat and some food, which she put into small bags and packed into the panniers on the back of the bike Morwyn had found for her. She was sent on her way with a curt 'Good luck' and an awkward pat on her shoulder. Sarah got on the bike and, shakily at first, headed off down the road.

Chapter V
Bones

Tom woke up with a pounding head and a feeling of lead in his body. It seemed to take a long time to surface properly — distant sounds began to creep into his consciousness, followed by the awareness of half-light. Was it early morning or evening? He seemed to have lost all sense of time. In one sense it was as if he'd just gone to sleep, but somehow, he knew that a lot of time had passed. When he managed to become properly awake, he propped himself up on one elbow and looked out the window. He was fairly sure that night was approaching — there were no birds singing and the quality of light was different to the morning. He could hear someone moving around the living room, so he got up and shakily tried a couple of steps towards Morwyn's room. He almost fell as his head swam and his stomach rolled — crap, he felt awful! He leaned on the door frame, and, once he got his balance, managed to walk out to the living room. Morwyn was standing by the table. When she noticed his presence, she turned to him, quickly arranging her face into a look of frustration.

"So you've decided to wake up at last! You've wasted two whole days and you didn't even manage to say goodbye to your friend."

"What?"

"Sarah got tired of waiting for you — she's left to try to

find her way back home," Morwyn said, nastily. "I was just waiting for you to wake to tell you I have to go out for the night and that you'll be alone. Don't wait up!" She strode across the room, her voluminous skirt billowing behind her, like a ship's sail gathering wind.

As she slammed the door and drew the bolts, Tom felt like he'd been hit in the chest. He let out a gasp and sank down onto the couch. He started counting backwards from fifty, as his sister Leah had taught him to do when he was anxious. He couldn't do it — he was feeling so bad! Sarah had gone! Just as he started to get used to someone — he'd let himself like her! And she was the only one who could understand what had happened to him. Why had she bothered to save him from the river? She should have left him to drown, then he wouldn't have to feel bad ever again. What was the point in being here, wherever 'here' was? He'd thought that at least they were in it together and would find out what was happening, and how to get away. He clenched his hands at his sides, so tight they started to ache, in the hope that that might stop him feeling the pain in his chest. He felt himself going a little dizzy, which sometimes happened when things got really bad, almost as if he phased out of himself to a place where he didn't hurt so much.

Just then, he heard tapping on the window. Hermione! Stupid cat — he didn't want to see her. He didn't want to feel good about anything, because everyone and everything ended up betraying him. He went over to the window and opened it to shout at her, "Go away! I don't want you here! Just go!" He pushed the window to close it, but Hermione was too quick for him and with one leap was in the house, and up on the table. He saw that his hand was near a pottery bowl and picked it up and threw it at her. It glanced off her side and smashed into the window, shattering glass all over the table and floor. Tom looked at it in dismay. He hadn't meant to let his anger take over — he just felt so bad! He saw that Hermione was crouched under the table looking at him warily. He felt devastated that he could be so mean and destructive, and ran to his room, throwing himself down on the bed, where he sobbed himself to sleep.

He woke a few hours later feeling strangely peaceful, with his arms wrapped around something warm, soft and vibrating. As he surfaced from a sleepy haze, he realised it was Hermione, purring gently. He patted her and told her how sorry he was. He could feel tears welling up, so he sat up and watched her as she washed her paws, then rubbed the right one over her right ear. She then put her paw down on something on the pillow, moving it towards him. He didn't immediately register what she was doing until she moved it again, closer. He then saw a small, folded up piece of paper with imprints from her teeth across it — she must have been carrying it in her mouth, but he was so upset when she'd arrived that he hadn't noticed. He unfolded it and flattened it out — it was a note from Sarah:

Dear Tom,

 I'm so sorry I've had to leave you. Morwyn has told me that you're seriously ill and the only way we can save you is if I find a remedy for her. Hermione tells me (yes, I know you'll smirk at that) that she is lying and that she wants me to find the remedy for her own purposes, that she has actually been giving you a sleeping draught and knows that I'll do it to save you. I figure that I have to do it to save us both and find a way out of this mess. Please stay here, pretend to be really upset with me for leaving you and lay low until I get back. Hermione will be with you — please trust her and know that I'll return for you. Watch out for Morwyn.

Wait for me,
Sarah

So, Sarah hadn't abandoned him! A flood of relief washed over him and he reached over and picked up Hermione, holding her close to his body, burying his face in her fur. His eyes started to fill up again, but this time because someone really cared about him. He hoped that now he would have the courage to deal with whatever happened until Sarah returned. He knew that he was quite strong really, but when he got upset everything else disappeared under panic and a dread that seemed to overwhelm him. With Hermione in his arms, he lay back and slipped into a light sleep. In a half dream state, it seemed as if Hermione was comforting him and was saying 'don't worry, I'll be here for you'. He had the impression that she would return through the window at night when Morwyn wasn't there, so he should leave it open; also, that she would take the note so Morwyn wouldn't find it. What a strangely real dream...

*

When Morwyn opened the door, the first thing she noticed was the broken window. So Tom was furious — her plan was working. She needed to make sure he stayed alive — he was her insurance to get the girl to co-operate, but that didn't mean she couldn't use him for her own purposes and maybe have a little fun with him in the meantime. She moved quietly through the rooms to where he was lying asleep on his bed. She drew a careful breath, then yelled, "Wake up! What have you done? You've broken the window and my work. Get up at once!"

Tom woke with a start to see Morwyn looming over him, her face enraged and contorted. He remembered a saying of his grandmother's: 'You'd better be careful, if the wind changes, you'll be stuck like that'. If the wind changed on Morwyn she'd look like one of those grimacing gargoyles at the entrance to the Notre Dame. He'd seen them on a documentary on TV and thought how hideous they were. As he quickly clambered out of bed, he knew he ought to be scared, yet somehow knowing the truth about what she was up to meant she wasn't as scary as Gerald. He'd escaped from that bully — he'd handle whatever happened with Morwyn.

Since she'd gone back to her room once she saw she'd frightened him awake, he took a moment to pull on some clean clothes and pull up the bed cover. He felt more secure if he had things ordered. He realised, though, that since he'd been here, it hadn't even occurred to him to use his rituals for eating — that must have been about Gerald.

"Get a move on! You've got work to do," Morwyn yelled out to him from the other room.

He went out through her bedroom to the living room, where she was standing with a brush and shovel, which she thrust at him. He started cleaning up the shards of pottery and glass, first from the floor, then from amongst her work on the table.

When he got to the figurines, he almost burst out laughing — quite a few of them were gargoyles — how funny that she'd been moulding herself without even knowing! He knew she didn't really look like one; she was just a normal looking woman, but in that moment of anger she'd suddenly seemed so... sort of twisted. Maybe that was a moment of seeing what was really inside her. Sarah would know, if only she was here — she seemed really good at seeing beyond the surface of things.

When he finished, Morwyn was sitting at the table with a cup of tea and some bread near her hand, and an open book in front of her. His stomach rumbled but she didn't offer him anything, brusquely telling him that his job for the day was to dig and extract clay for her pottery, and if he did what she asked of him, he could eat and have some time to himself later. She took a key from her pocket and unlocked the door, beckoning him to the edge where the ladder was already extended down to the ground.

"I'll go first, you follow. No tricks or you'll regret it."

She clambered over the edge and disappeared. Tom hesitated, then followed her. It was momentarily disconcerting as he turned and lowered his foot to the first rung, and felt the ladder swing out beneath him, but he continued and made his way down to the ground, where Morwyn was waiting for him.

She indicated that he was to follow her across the grass to the brick shed, where opening a green wooden door in the front revealed a small space that contained gardening tools.

"What's on the other side of the shed?" There were no windows, but there was a chimney in the roof.

"It's a kiln for firing my pottery. Here, take this." She thrust a spade into his hands, then pulled out two sturdy looking sacks, slung them over her shoulder and shut the door.

"Follow me."

She strode off towards the trees that surrounded the clearing. Tom had to half jog to keep up with her. The trees on this side looked a bit like pine — there were needles on the ground that softened the sound of their footfalls and they gave off a nice, woody scent. They walked in silence for about ten minutes before breaking out of the trees to a grassy bank with a river beyond.

"This is the River Dearth — it goes down through the town." Morwyn threw the sacks down the bank to the pebbles at the edge of the river and neatly vaulted down beside them. She held out a hand for the spade and Tom made his way down to join her. He stood at the side of the river, for a moment lost in the warmth of the day, the sound of the river flowing over the stones, and the fresh smell of water and foliage.

"Stop daydreaming, you've got work to do!"

Tom snapped out of his reverie and followed her a short way up the river. Morwyn stopped at a place where the river bank had been exposed either by a slip or previous digging — he could see a seam of pale clay between the grassy bank and the river bed. She threw the bags on the ground.

"You've got two hours to fill the sacks. Don't try to run away — there's nowhere for you to go and I'll be watching you anyway. I'll know if you move more than twenty strides from here in any direction."

"What are you going to do?"

"Never you mind, just do your job. If you're thirsty, the

river water is pure and good to drink."

She made her way back up the bank and into the trees. Tom wondered what she was up to, but didn't want to push his luck the first day by doing something stupid to test her. He dipped his hands in the water and had a long, cool drink before opening a sack near the clay bank and starting to dig at the seam. As he swung the spade, he was glad Gerald had made him do so much in the garden. It was hard work, but he was fit and agile despite the events of the past couple of days.

It seemed to take forever to fill each sack and they were incredibly heavy to shift when they were full. When he finally finished, he guessed that it had taken him a bit more than an hour and a half. Hot and sweaty, he took off his shoes and walked into the river. He dipped his hands into the water and threw it over his face and hair. It felt so good, so cool, that he pulled off his shorts and T-shirt, waded out a little and lay down in a natural pool in the rocks. The water was cold after the heat from working, but it was incredibly peaceful, gazing up at the blue sky and listening to the sounds of the river and the birds. He roused himself — she would be back before long and he wanted to be dressed when she got there. He felt too vulnerable to deal with her without all his clothes on. He stood up and shook himself like a dog, watching drops of water from his hair spin out and hit the water with soft splashes. He dried himself with his T-shirt — it would dry soon enough in the sun, and pulled his shorts and T-shirt back on.

He wandered a short distance up the edge of the river, until he saw something pale under the pebbles. He nudged at it with his foot and as the pebbles shifted, he saw what looked like bone. He knelt down and cleared the pebbles away — it was the end of a bone, something like a knee or an elbow. He'd seen them on the crime dramas he watched on TV. He grabbed the end and gave it a pull. The ground holding it underneath shifted and gave it up into his hand. It wasn't that big, not an adult's bone — he guessed it would have belonged to someone youngish like him — an arm — he couldn't remember what that bone was called — the one that went from the shoulder to the elbow. He suddenly felt sick and scared. Did that mean other kids had been here before him, working for Morwyn? Had they died? Had she killed them? The bone suddenly felt too hot to hold and he threw it up the river, where it sank beneath the surface. He felt horrible and sat down on the bank. There was no way he was going to try anything silly today. He'd maybe have to push it a bit tomorrow or she'd wonder why he didn't try to escape, unless she thought he was a wimp, but he couldn't face it for now. His breathing was ragged and his heart was racing. He worked hard at deep breathing and counting to try to get it back to normal before Morwyn returned.

*

When Morwyn left Tom at the riverbank she walked back into the trees, then turned left down a rough track that took her a little downstream. She made her way back to the river to where there was another exposed seam of clay in the bank. She pulled a small trowel and bowl out of the pocket of her skirt and carefully extracted a couple of trowel loads of clay, avoiding twigs and debris. Putting the clay in the bowl, she added water and worked the clay to a smooth paste with her hands. When it reached the right consistency, she smeared it over her face and neck. This clay had particularly good rejuvenating properties — she'd needed to apply it more and more frequently lately. She was feeling increasingly desperate and didn't know what she would do if Sarah failed at her task. The elixir was her last hope to prevent the rapid onset of aging that she'd kept at bay for so long. She would not grow old!

She found a tree with a low fork in its branches and pulled herself up. Seated in the fork she could see Tom working on the bank through a narrow gap in the trees. She didn't think he would try to escape yet. He was thoughtful and would plan it first. He also gave off a strong whiff of fear. She could use that, though she had to tread carefully until Sarah returned. He was her guarantee for Sarah's compliance. She settled in to wait, letting her mind wander to her last night with Willard and the double pleasure she'd had in enjoying his company, while at the same time experiencing the delicious feeling that came from the thought of deceiving and bettering him. Her thoughts drifted, and in a half sleep state found herself in a memory from long ago…

"Morwyn, Morwyn, what are you doing? Get away from that mirror. You can't make a silk purse out of a sow's ear! Come and help me with my dress." Her mother was turning in front of a full-length mirror, admiring the deep red dress that hugged her body, showing off her seductive curves. She was holding up her heavy, dark hair, exposing the back of her neck for Morwyn to do up a hook that would hold the plunging neckline in place. She was going out with yet another unknown man for the evening, a regular event since her father's mysterious death a little over a year ago. He'd just kind of faded away. One week fine, the next unable to eat, lethargic, and then he was gone! He'd never really protected her from her mother's rages, but he'd been kind to her, when he wasn't either absent or trying to appease her mother. Now, there was no one there for her.

When she was little, she'd been dressed up and shown off like a little princess, but when she reached puberty and started getting breasts and her period, everything changed. Her mother's violent temper started being directed at her — she obviously offended her in every way. Her legs were too long, her hair too unruly, her face too ugly. She was stupid, she was smart-mouthed, she was slow, she was apathetic, she was pathetic... When she turned thirteen, she'd stopped her going to school, saying that there was no point. She would never have a man interested in her, she was too ugly, so if she was going to be stuck with her forever, she might as well start learning what to do now.

As she secured her mother's dress, she heard the front door close and footsteps on the stairs. Her grandmother. She was 'keeping an eye on her' for the evening while her mother was out. Goodness only knows what she thought she would do alone — she was never allowed any space. Her grandmother was frightening. When she was there, tension crackled in the room between her and her mother. They were locked into some sort of dance together that kept them playing out their games of love and hate, a weird and destructive connection that they couldn't let go of. Tonight, her mother told her that Morwyn needed taking down a peg or two as she waltzed out the door into the night, causing her grandmother to laugh in a particularly nasty way that made the hair on her arms bristle.

Her grandmother started off pleasantly enough. She made her a hot chocolate and sat her down at the table while she busied herself doing something in the kitchen. Her skin prickled — she didn't trust her being nice. Normally, at best, she was ignored. She started to feel drowsy. Her head flopped to one side and she realised she couldn't move it back. She couldn't move anything! She tried to say something but nothing worked! In a daze, she saw her grandmother coming towards her with a crooked smile on her face that looked evil. She went behind her and came back brandishing a large pair of scissors used for cutting material.

"Think you're better than us, do you? Well, it's time we slapped any smugness and silly ideas off your ugly face."

She started hacking at her hair, letting great swathes of it drop to the floor. Morwyn tried to scream and nothing came out of her mouth. She screamed so loudly in her head, in such total helplessness and despair, that eventually she blacked out. When she woke up, she was lying on the floor, the kitchen was clean, her grandmother had gone and she wondered if it had been a bad dream. But when she got up and put her hand to her head, there was nothing there. Just a few tufts and some sore patches — her fingers came away sticky. She raced into the hall and looked into the mirror. She looked shorn and mutilated. She opened her mouth and screamed and screamed, fainting and falling to the floor.

Morwyn came back to the present, overcome with shame and rage. In her fury, she started scratching at her arms and legs, and when that didn't hurt enough, she broke a stick off a tree and started gouging at her skin, deeper and deeper. Anything to make her feel physical pain rather than remembering the horror she'd just revisited. She looked up and realised with a start that Tom wasn't in view. She was furious. *If they don't do what I want them to, I'll crush them! I'll squeeze them so hard that first their hearts, then their eyes, will pop.* She realised she'd attacked the inside of her arm so hard that the stick had broken off and a piece was left embedded in her skin. It was really painful and she started to climb down from her perch in the tree to see to it, just as Tom came back into view. She saw him pulling on his shirt — he must have been in the river.

She made her way down to the river below the tree, pulled the piece of stick out of her arm with her fingernails and bound the wound tightly with a piece of material from the bottom of her skirt. She then took her clothes off and immersed herself in the river, watching the rivulets of blood flowing down her arms and legs lighten and wash away. Her mask washed off easily, and getting out of the river she shook herself free of the water and of the memories she'd had. By the time she was re-clothed, they were pushed back down into the dark place they'd emerged from, as if they'd never been.

*

By the time Morwyn emerged from the trees, Tom was feeling calm again. When he first saw her, part of him registered that she looked a little different. She had scratches on her arms and something tied around her wrist — maybe she'd fallen and grazed herself. She also looked fresher somehow, but that was quickly forgotten as he saw her hoist the two sacks onto her shoulders as if they only weighed a fraction more than they had when they were empty.

"Carry the spade," she barked as she marched off along the path through the trees. Once again, he found himself jogging to keep up, even though the bags must be incredibly heavy. When they reached the clearing, she dropped the sacks by the shed and went around to the kiln door. She pulled out two large, slotted trays, which she deposited on the ground near him.

"Spread the clay out on the trays so it will dry in the sun. When you've finished you can have something to eat."

It took him half an hour to lay out all the clods of clay. By the time he was finished he was hot, hungry and a little light-headed. He'd had nothing to eat since the previous evening and it must be into the early afternoon by now. Morwyn called out to him from the deck of the treehouse, "Come up if you've finished, and pull the ladder up after you."

On reaching the living room he found her sitting at the table with water, bread, cheese and fruit. So, more of the same then! But when he started eating, he realised he was so famished it tasted like the best food in the world. He tried to make some conversation by asking where she got her water from, to which her terse reply was that it was a thermal region and she used the underground steam to drive a pump that took water from the stream to the house. She then told him he could rest for an hour and that he would then spend the afternoon chopping firewood.

*

It was a long and exhausting day. He had chopped and split wood for what felt like hours, then stacked half of it behind the shed and the rest on the platform. He then carried it from the platform to the wood baskets either side of the fireplace. Morwyn had given him some sort of meaty broth with bread to mop it up, then locked him in and left for whatever her nightly business was.

He now lay on the bed feeling shattered. Every bone and muscle in his body ached and felt exhausted, and the pads on his palms and fingers were hot and blistered. He wondered what Sarah was doing and whether she was okay. He heard Hermione's soft footsteps and she jumped up beside him and leaned into him. He stroked her, but when his hand started to throb, he rested it palm up on the bedcover and closed his eyes. He felt something hot and rough on his palm, like sandpaper. He yelped, but when he looked up, Hermione was sitting with one paw on his wrist, the other over his fingers, gently holding him down. He realised the rasping was actually quite soothing and let her continue. He then noticed that where she'd been licking, the redness was retreating back towards the blisters. *What?* he thought, *that's amazing!* At the same time though, it seemed kind of freaky — in his world he could never have accepted that something like this could happen!

When she'd finished with both hands, she washed herself, then snuggled up against him, purring. With one arm around her, Tom drifted off into a relaxed sleep, feeling something warm and tender that was unfamiliar, wonderful and, if he'd been more awake, a bit disturbing. As he was floating into a half-sleep, he imagined that Hermione was saying 'Well done' to him for managing the day. She told him that no matter what difficulties the next few days brought, to trust that she would be there for him, and to keep a cool head and warm heart.

Chapter VI
Sarah's Tasks

The gravel on the road from Morwyn's house was even rougher than Sarah remembered from the car ride, and it took a while to get used to navigating around potholes and wheel ruts. The first part wasn't so bad, but when she got to two sharp corners in the middle of a copse of trees, the gravel was so loose that her bike started to wobble. She over-corrected and the front wheel dug into a large piece of stone that stopped the bike suddenly, plunging her over the handlebars, landing with a thud on the ground. All the air seemed to be thumped out of her chest, as she landed spread-eagled on the gravel, with her right leg still straddled over the bike and her left caught underneath it.

She slowly picked herself up, leaving the bike on the ground, and looked down at her torn leggings. They seemed to have stopped too much damage to her knees — there was a bit of blood seeping from grazes on each of them, but her palms stung like crazy. The grazes there were quite deep and were weeping blood through a layer of dirt that needed to be cleaned somehow... Sarah remembered that Morwyn had put a container of water into a pannier, but for the moment she just needed to sit down. Walking unsteadily to the side of the road where there was a grassy verge, she lowered herself to the ground, shaking all over with shock. She leaned back and closed her eyes, breathing deeply and trying to calm her nerves to find a more stable place inside herself. Eventually, she had the strength to sit up and go over to her bike to find the water and clean her hands. Not having anything to bind them with, she used every last ounce of her determination to get back on the bike and continue on her journey.

It was much easier once she got to the main road. There the gravel was compacted into a firm surface and she could ride much more freely. It was a warm day and Sarah was glad that Morwyn had given her some cooler tops to wear. Riding in itself was all right, but she'd have enjoyed it a lot more if it wasn't for the feeling of dread lurking in her stomach. She didn't come across many people — just a few cars a bit like Morwyn's. They travelled quietly too, and she wondered if Tom would know why — it seemed like the sort of thing he would know. *I wonder if he's okay and whether he'll get the note from Hermione*, she thought. At one point, she came across a group of boys riding bikes in the opposite direction. They whistled and called out to her. Embarrassing! She put her head down and carried on cycling.

The countryside was fairly flat, but she could see mountains far in the distance. A row of trees that reminded her of poplars meandered along with the direction of the road a little to her left — she remembered seeing on the map that they followed the river that passed through Hunterdale. As she drew nearer to the town the road became busier and she started to see open-backed trucks passing her, carrying straw, poles and canvas, going in the same direction as her towards the town. She imagined they'd be heading there to set up for tomorrow's market.

Sarah only stopped once to have some water and check the map, so after a couple of hours she could see signs of the approaching town, with a growing number of dwellings, mostly houses, sheds and small plots of land to begin with, but the housing quickly became denser. They were mostly made of stone or brick, a few of timber, clustering either side of the road. Soon, she spotted a curved stone bridge that arched up and over the river, with sides about three feet high. The road veered to the left as she approached it, and then suddenly, she was riding up onto the bridge, and at the top of the curve found herself overlooking the town of Hunterdale on the other side of the fast-flowing River Dearth. She stopped and leaned against the side for a moment to get her bearings.

Oh wow, what a cool looking town. It was nestled in between the river and what looked like a forest, with the mountains forming a backdrop in the distance. It looked similar in a lot of ways to a small English town out in the countryside, with stone houses and narrow streets just wide enough for vehicles. What seemed a bit strange, though, was that steam was coming out of the chimneys from many of the houses and buildings. It wasn't smoke — it was much thinner and clean looking. It was too warm for fires anyway, so it must be steam. She got back on her bike and slowly free-wheeled her way down the other side of the bridge. The road she could see leading from the bridge straight into the town, would be the one Morwyn told her to take, called Market Road. It led into the town square where the market was held.

Once Sarah was over the bridge, she found that the roads were cobbled and rather bumpy. She decided to dismount and wheeled the bike across a road at right angles to the bridge, and into Market Road. It was bustling, with lots of people going about their chores, not taking any notice of her. Without much of a footpath it was a bit rough, but she stuck to the edge and walked the bike up the road. The houses seemed to be built high off the ground, with steps up to the first floor. She wondered whether maybe the river sometimes flooded and whether they could keep anything in their basements. A block before the road opened out to the town square, there was a sign for Rose Road, where she knew she had to turn left to get to Dervla's house. She swallowed, feeling nervous, and wiped her sweaty palms on her leggings, wincing when she remembered too late, as they caught on the fabric, that her palms were grazed.

Sarah walked the bike along Rose Road as she looked for Number 27. It was a tall, two storey, narrow house, free-standing but sandwiched between two others of a similar style. It was made of grey stone and had a steeply pitched roof clad with shingles. She leaned her bicycle against the front steps and, with a sense of trepidation, climbed up the steps to the red front door. She knocked on it using the large brass knocker shaped like a lion's head. She could hear the loud knock reverberating inside the house. Clutching her hands tightly in fists at her side, she waited for Dervla to come to the door.

Through the glass she could see a figure approaching and the door swung open to reveal a woman of medium height, a bit younger than Morwyn, with jet-black hair, dark eyes and olive skin. It crossed her mind that she was kind of attractive, in a witchy sort of way.

"Yes?"

"Hello, I'm Sarah. Morwyn sent me to see if you could help me."

"Morwyn? I find that hard to believe." Dervla went to shut the door on her.

"Oh please… It's really important. It's a matter of life and death for a friend of mine."

Dervla hesitated, standing in the doorway with her hand on the door knob, ready to close the door.

"She said I was to ask you for a golden thread, a place to stay for the night and to be able to leave my bike here for a couple of days."

"And why would I do that?"

"She says you owe her a favour."

"Hmmm." She looked fierce and grumpy, but she swung the door further open and stepped back so that Sarah could walk past her into the hallway.

Inside it was dark, in a delicious rather than a scary way — it was like she was entering some sort of magical grotto. The walls were painted a deep burgundy, with recesses that reflected low light shining from lamps; a heavy chandelier lit with candles rather than electric lights hung down from the high ceiling, and she could smell something musky like incense. A deep red and black rug stretched along the hallway over terracotta tiles, leading to a lighter, more open area that turned out to be a living room and kitchen. The living room walls were lined with books, plants and interesting-looking art

— under other circumstances Sarah would have loved to stop and explore the room, but Dervla was looking at her expectantly. She realised she must have said something to her.

"I'm sorry, I missed what you said."

"I said that I'll give you what you want, but it might not be as easy as you think. Come with me." She led the way to a room opening off the living room that may have originally been intended to be a bedroom. It had a fireplace with chairs and a small table clustered around it, a frame that looked like it held a half-completed tapestry, and in the far corner a large wardrobe. What drew Sarah's attention though, was a stand with a large brown bird tethered to it.

"It's a hawk. Don't touch him, he'll attack you — he doesn't like people."

The bird's eyes followed Sarah as she walked further into the room.

"He's beautiful!"

"Come over here." Dervla indicated the wardrobe. "You won't be needing a place to sleep for the night. You're going to be fully occupied!" She yanked the wardrobe door open and masses of skeins of thread tumbled out. They spread in all directions over the floor, every colour imaginable, some in bundles, some single, all tangled together in a mess.

"If you can find a gold thread in there, you can have it. I have things to do. I'd prefer that you keep to yourself — I don't like company… You'll find water in the kitchen. Good luck with that!" she said wryly, nodding at the mess of threads as she went out and shut the door.

As the door closed, Sarah sat down on the floor, suddenly feeling exhausted and overwhelmed by the events of the last few days and the task in front of her. She put her head between her knees and started crying. If all felt totally unmanageable and she just wanted to run away. After a while though, it started to seep into her consciousness that she could hear a jangling sound. Lifting her head, she saw the hawk sitting on the far end of his stand pecking at the chain around his leg. She sniffed and rubbed her hand over her eyes. She noticed then that the chain was tangled and he couldn't reach the far side of the stand, where there was a small platform with a bowl on it. Pulling herself to her feet Sarah hesitantly approached the hawk, hoping he wouldn't peck her. Picking up the bowl of water, she tentatively held it out towards him, willing him to keep away from her fingers. She needn't have worried — he immediately dipped his beak repeatedly into the water, taking a very long drink.

"Goodness, you're thirsty. I wonder how long it is since you've been seen to. I wonder if you're hungry too — just letting you know, there's no way I'm finding mice for you to eat! Maybe I'll just have to free you instead."

She put the water bowl back and had a look at the chain. It was so tangled she didn't know how she'd free it without holding the bird, which she wasn't keen to do. She saw that it was attached to his foot with a locking ring.

"I guess I'd better search for the key then — hopefully she's left it in here somewhere." She wandered over to the small table, but then heard the hawk rattling his chain. She turned to look at him and he was bobbing his head in the direction of the mantelpiece. She went over to it and, sure enough, the key was sitting there beside a candle.

"Oh, you're so clever. I wonder if you understand what

I'm saying to you… Don't peck me, I'm trying to help." She tentatively lifted her hands to his feet and gently held the one with the ring on it, while she inserted the key and turned it. The lock clicked and the ring fell off his foot. He immediately gave her a huge fright by hopping onto her shoulder. His grip was firm but didn't hurt. He then carefully lowered his head and gently stroked his beak across her cheek. Tears came to her eyes again, this time because of his obvious gratitude and affection. She put her hand up and lightly touched the soft feathers on his head, then carefully crouched down and suggested that he jump off so she could go and check where Dervla was — she'd have to be well out of the way if she was going to let the hawk go.

Sarah opened the door and went out into the living room, jumping when she saw Dervla sitting at the table reading a book. She was looking at her over her glasses, but didn't say anything.

"I'm just getting some water."

Dervla ignored her, turning a page and making it clear she didn't want to talk to her.

Sarah returned to the room and closed the door.

"Looks like we're going to have to wait until the coast is clear in the morning. I've got a huge night ahead of me."

She sat cross-legged on the floor and started sifting through the threads. She decided it would be easier if she organised them first and started dropping similar colours together in piles, untangling them as she went.

"I wish I could talk to you properly — I'm pretty sure you can understand me."

He made some quiet clacking noises. She wondered if she could tune into him like she did to Hermione and lay down and closed her eyes, trying to 'feel' into him. After a while, the noises he was making started to half make sense as scratchy words. She thought she understood him to be saying he would help, but in her exhaustion, she fell into a deep sleep right where she was on the floor.

*

When Sarah woke it was dark, but she could hear some birds chirping faintly in the distance and presumed it was nearly dawn. Sitting up, she could just make out the shape of the hawk perched on the table watching her. She felt panicky — she'd not intended to fall asleep — however would she find the thread now before morning? Morwyn had told her to arrive at Willard's house soon after nine to make sure he was away at the market for the maximum time, while she found the container. She fumbled her way over to the door, hoping for a light switch, and, sure enough, her fingers found one. She switched it on, then when she turned back into the room gave a gasp. All the threads were sorted into tidy piles not only of like colour, but also types of thread. Sitting on the table beside the hawk were two threads gleaming golden in the light.

"Oh, my goodness, that's amazing! Did you do that?"

The hawk inclined his head.

"You're wonderful. How can I thank you enough?"

The hawk made some sounds that Sarah asked him to repeat while she tried to tune into his speech again. She was fairly sure he said 'You already have by setting me free'. She said it back to him and he bobbed his head again. She felt really moved and went over to sit by him on the table, where he let her gently stroke the back of his head with her index finger. His feathers were so soft, almost downy, and up close not just brown, but a rich mixture of shades of colour from nutmeg through to a tawny orange, black, an underlay of cream and even slithers of white. He had white markings around his eyes.

"What are you called? Do you have a name?"

"The one good human I've known called me Ryder."

"Ryder?"

"It means warrior."

"That's a good name... so that's what I'll call you. I really want to know how you ended up with Dervla, but we need to get away from here while she's hopefully still asleep. I'm going to go out to the kitchen and if she's not there, I'll come back for you and we'll leave." She picked up the threads and went out the door. The house was still dark and silent, so she returned for Ryder, who hopped onto her shoulder and they quietly left the house. Once they were outside, he flew to a tree, and waited while Sarah got her bike and wheeled it back along the road. While it would have been easier for her to leave it there, she didn't want Dervla to do anything with it out of spite for setting Ryder free, and didn't want to risk seeing her again when she returned for it. She was hoping that if they were out of sight, they would stay out of mind. She wanted to set as much distance between her and Dervla as she could before she woke up, so she walked quickly with the bike down the road, heading for the town square, checking to make sure Ryder was following.

The dawn was just breaking — the morning calls of birds were getting louder, the sky was streaked with a pearly grey, suffused light and, as she approached the town square, she could hear the clatter of people setting up their wares for the market. She was looking for somewhere she could sit unnoticed for a while to have a conversation with Ryder and wait for nine o'clock. He'd flown up into the sky when he saw she was safely away from the house, and she could see him from afar, wheeling in great arcs through the air — she presumed he was keeping an eye out for where she was going. On the far side of the square, she could see a cluster of trees and shrubs, and decided to head over to them so that she could hide her bike.

As Sarah walked around the sides of the town square, she could hear conversations and banter between people as they organised their food and crafts for sale. They sounded friendly and inviting, as if they knew each other well. Her stomach rumbled as she caught a whiff of the wonderful smell of freshly baked bread, and realised she hadn't eaten since before she left Morwyn's the previous day. A small dog came up to her and sniffed at her legs — he was a scruffy, caramel coloured terrier with black-button, sparkling eyes and a wagging tail. She patted him on the head and asked him where his owner was, looking around her, before seeing a woman hurrying towards them.

"Scruff, where have you been? I thought I'd lost you. Don't bother that girl — she's not going to give you any food!"

Sarah smiled. "He's no bother, he's very cute. And I don't have any food that he'd be interested in, just an apple!"

"So, you haven't tried the wonderful pastries from the stall on the other side of the square? Here, have one." She handed her a crisp pastry from a bag — it had apricot in the middle and was glazed with shiny syrup — it smelled divine.

"Thank you so much, that's wonderful."

The woman wandered off with Scruff, and Sarah continued to make her way between stalls towards the trees she'd seen. Once there, she walked along the path at the side of the trees a little until she found a bench, and, propping the bike up alongside her, sat down to eat her pastry. It was delicious, very delicate, flaky and not too sweet.

As she sat there watching people starting to arrive at the square to make the most of the early traders already open for business, she was thinking about how generous people could be even when they didn't know her; also, about Hermione saying that help would come to her when she needed it. How true that had been of Ryder. She'd have to hold that thought close to her over the next few hours, because she was really scared of going to Willard's. She'd been too busy to give it much thought, but now the reality that she was going to go into someone's house, uninvited, and steal something, made her feel weak with worry. She heard a soft cry and looked up to see Ryder sinking down from a tree to stand beside her on the bench. Just the sight of him made her feel better and she took a deep breath to steady herself.

"Hello, Ryder, I'm so glad you're here. I'm terrified about what I have to do next and I wonder whether you'll stay around long enough to make sure I'm safe... I have to go to someone's house and take a container without them knowing — could you stay close and warn me if the owner comes back?" He inclined his head and made a clacking noise. "Thank you! I have to think it through properly, but we've got some time yet before I have to go, so tell me about your 'good' human and how you came to be a captive of Dervla's."

It was hard for Sarah to stay tuned into Ryder's way of speech — it was squawky and sometimes erratic compared to Hermione, a bit like the scratchiness of listening to her grandfather's antique gramophone, but after a while she managed to make out his story. He told her that when he was young, he'd been trained to hunt by a kind man called Cathal. He'd been with him for several years, was well looked after and had a lot of freedom, unlike most others of his kind used for hunting. Cathal trusted that he would return for food, so he didn't leave him locked up or hooded. When Cathal died suddenly in an accident, his neighbour took over his property and tricked Ryder, keeping him captive until he got sick of him, selling him to a man called Willard, who then gave him to Dervla as a gift. Dervla didn't really know what to do with him and he'd been stuck in her room for several months, as if he was some sort of pet to put on show. She didn't know how to handle him, so she couldn't risk letting him fly. When Sarah told him that it was Willard's house she was going to break into, Ryder said grimly that he wasn't a good person and that he was very happy to help.

*

When the market was properly underway, Sarah looked around to try to get an idea of the time. She wished she'd been wearing her watch when she found her way into this strange world. She missed it more than her iPhone, which was funny, because at home her mother was always worried that she couldn't be without it, saying that 'her generation' was too dependent on them. Yet since she'd been here, she hadn't really even noticed that she didn't have it, and certainly didn't need it — she was too preoccupied with surviving! Sarah could see though, from the clock on the tower of a large, cream stone building nearby that looked like it might be the town hall, that she still had a bit of time. She and Ryder had planned to leave close to nine. It was fortunate that Ryder knew what Willard looked like, because he could watch out for him and keep him in sight while Sarah made her way to his house. If things went wrong, Ryder said he'd find a way to warn her, and if everything went to plan, they would meet up in the belt of trees behind where they were now. She'd taken the bike and concealed it there, leaving all her things hidden in the cavity of a tree trunk, except for the sleeping draught and the thread, which she put in her pocket.

Just before nine, when the market place was filling up with people, Ryder, who was now perched in the tree above her, flapped his wings to get her attention and jerked his head in the direction of the town hall. A tall, dark-haired man dressed in baggy trousers and some kind of waistcoat, had just entered the square and was making his way over to stalls on the opposite side. Sarah stood up and walked in the other direction, skirting behind the stalls around to the town hall. She turned left into the street directly before the building, the one Willard had just exited. Cross Street. It was a much nicer street than Dervla's; green and leafy with trees growing either side of a wide road and with a footpath either side. She walked down the street and across two intersections until she came to

Number 55.

Willard's house was made of the same grey stone as the ones either side of it, though it was smaller; a modest but neat single storey house with open, dark blue shutters and a door the same colour. She decided that the best thing was to be bold in case someone was looking, so she walked straight up the front steps and knocked on the door. All was quiet, so she turned back down the steps and followed the gravel path along the side of the house, through a small gate and found herself in the back garden. Sure enough, there was a small garden shed. She opened the door, which creaked on slightly rusting hinges, stood inside and ran her hand along the lintel above the door. Nothing. She tried again, thinking she must have missed it. Still nothing. She suddenly felt hot and sweaty and panicky. Where else could he have hidden it? She tried under the mat outside the door and under the pots beside it. With increasing panic, she started searching the shelf that extended along the walls around the room. It would be a huge job to look under all the bags of fertiliser and garden implements stacked on the floor... If she couldn't find it she might have to break a window — the thought made her feel sick! She sat down on the ground for a minute and breathed deeply, then started again at the other end of the shelf. She moved a box of slug repellent and her hand brushed against something metallic. She snatched it up and, sure enough, it was the key — it must have fallen off the lintel onto the end of the shelf. Sarah felt very shaky, but relieved, and made her way around to the front door again and inserted the key into the lock. It opened easily and she quickly slipped inside and closed the door, locking it behind her.

The door opened into a short vestibule with coat hooks on the wall on one side, then into an open living area with a couple of worn looking armchairs, bookcases and a fireplace. To her right there was a door that led into a large kitchen with enough room for a wooden table and chairs. She went into the room and could see a glass and a pitcher of something on the table and a single place setting, as if he was expecting to come back to have a meal. As a precaution, she took out the container of sleeping draught and emptied half of it into the pitcher, before going back to the living room. Moving on through the room she came to a short corridor with a low ceiling and rough brown matting covering the floor. It had one door to the left and three to the right. Pushing open the creaky door that was ajar on her right, she saw a small bedroom that looked unused. The next door, which was standing open, led to a scungy looking bathroom that definitely needed a clean! The last door on that side was shut and when she turned the handle it wouldn't budge — it was locked. Being so close to the bathroom it would be a tiny space, so maybe it led down to a basement.

Sarah went back and hesitantly entered the room on the other side of the corridor. She'd imagined it would be Willard's bedroom since it was the largest, and when she tentatively glanced around, it was as if she could feel Willard's presence in there, heavy and lingering. The room was sparsely furnished, with windows on two of the drab beige walls, and had an undefinable male smell, maybe coming from the untidy pile of clothes spilling off the end of one side of the large bed over a blanket box at its foot, and onto the floor. *Yuk, it smells stale*, she thought, wrinkling her nose. Looking around the room she could also see a bedside table and an old-fashioned wardrobe. And — against the wall that backed onto the corridor, there was a dresser, just as Morwyn had described it. Her eyes were immediately drawn to its top, and there it was: a small, carved wooden box, a rectangle of about five by four inches, standing about three inches high off the dresser. She stretched out her hand and ran her index finger over the pattern on the top — it was some sort of intricate design that radiated out from a central point.

"Clack, clack, clack." Sarah nearly jumped out of her skin. She looked over to the window the noise was coming from and saw that it was Ryder tapping on the glass with his beak. That was the signal that Willard was approaching. Why would he be back so early? Now that she was concentrating, she could hear the key in the lock of the front door. She looked around the room in a panic and her eyes fell on the wooden blanket box at the foot of the bed. Racing over to it, she lifted the lid, heavy with the weight of the clothes sprawled on it, and seeing that it had enough space for her, she scrambled in, curling herself up into a comma shape, letting the lid fall down into place above her.

It was completely dark. She couldn't even see her fingers in front of her eyes. She held her breath as someone entered the room and walked across to the dresser, then to the wardrobe, opening its creaking door. She could feel her heart pummelling against her ribs and blood rushing in her head, pushing against her eardrums with a whooshing sound. She slowly let out her breath, trying to be completely silent as she heard the person turn and leave the room. She had a moment where relief washed over her, before registering just where she was. She was enclosed, in a box, in a pitch-black place, and she didn't know how long for! If he didn't leave again, even if he drank from the pitcher immediately, she'd be there for a good half hour, and it might be much longer. How would she know without risking being seen? Would there be enough air in the box to last? Why was he back here so soon? Dervla must have warned him about her. What if she'd described what she looked like?

Suddenly, the box felt unbearably constricting, and she began to panic. She tried reasoning with herself that of course she could breathe, but she started gasping for air as complete terror of suffocation took her over. She wanted desperately to open the lid or kick out at the sides — it took every bit of self-control she had to stay still and silent. Her eyes were leaking tears and her mouth was so dry it felt as if her tongue was stuck to its roof. She tried to breathe deeply and regularly, and gradually she managed to bring herself back from the brink of falling into an abyss of churning, devouring fear. She slowly came back to being aware of her surroundings. All was quiet in the bedroom. In the box she was lying on some type of coarse fabric, and something hard was digging into her hip. She felt a bit cramped but thought she'd be able to stay curled up like this for a while. With that thought she experienced another surge of claustrophobia, but short-lived this time. She decided that if it happened again, she'd risk opening the lid of the box just a fraction to feel some air, and the thought that she had some control calmed her.

Her mind wandered to a time when she was little, before she started school, and she'd been playing at her best friend, Suzanne's, house. Suzanne had a brother a few years older who used to tease and annoy them. Her friend had a large dolls' house with a hinged roof so that they could play with their dolls and furniture from above. Once, her brother had dared Sarah to get into it, and had then closed the roof and sat on it so she couldn't get out. Even though she pleaded and cried he wouldn't give in. It had been completely terrifying. Even though she could breathe and it was light, the irrational fear that she couldn't get out the little doors or windows and was trapped, so consumed her that she'd peed in terror. When eventually he'd let her out, she felt so humiliated she couldn't tell her friend and had to secretly clean it out. She'd had to hide her knickers and invent an excuse to go home early. Her mum had found them stuffed behind a chest of drawers — even though she'd been really understanding, the terror and shame had remained with her for ages. Even now, it came back so easily and got all messed up with where she was now, and she found her heart pounding again. Sarah raised the box lid a fraction to let in a sliver of light and a tiny current of fresh air. She lay there breathing deeply, waiting for the courage to be able to go and find out where Willard was.

*

After what felt like a lifetime, with everything remaining still and silent, Sarah dared to slowly open the box and creep out across the bedroom to the door. Everything was quiet, other than her heart, which felt like it was going to pound right out of her chest. He wasn't in the living room, so she inched her way towards the kitchen and, from several feet away, could see him in the kitchen, asleep, slumped with his head resting on his arms. The glass was beside his right elbow, half full of an amber coloured liquid that he must have poured from the jug. He had dark, dishevelled, shoulder-length hair streaked with silver. She could see his shoulders rising and falling — he was breathing! Thank goodness he was alive; she didn't want a dead body on her conscience. He stirred and her heart leapt into her mouth, almost making her gasp. She froze and was about to inch backwards again, but he relaxed back into a deep sleep. His movement, though, revealed a belt around his waist, beneath a well-worn leather jerkin, and she could see a ring of keys fastened to it. Did she dare to get close enough to take them? She stood indecisively at the entrance to the kitchen for ages, planning what she would do if he woke, but eventually she decided to grasp her courage and make a move. Inching forwards, she reached out her hand towards them, holding her breath, but he didn't move, so she slid the ring around until it unhooked from his belt and with it grasped in her hand, she got out of the kitchen as fast as she could.

Rushing now, she went back into the bedroom, picked up the box, using the small key to unlock it, and removed the golden casket from inside. Part of her would like to have taken the box — she was very glad she hadn't had to smash it as Morwyn had suggested, but she thought that if she left it, it may take Willard longer to realise she'd been there and that the container was gone. She carefully put it back on the top of the dresser, trying to remember exactly where it had been when she first saw it.

She was then all set to rush for the front door, but as she looked at the key ring in her hand, she wondered what the other keys were for. The large one was clearly the key for his front door… Maybe one of the others was for the door down at the end of the corridor. Her curiosity got the better of her — since he was so fast asleep, surely it wouldn't hurt if she took a moment to see what was in there?

Walking quietly, on tiptoes, even though she knew Willard couldn't hear her, she went to the end of the corridor and tried one of the keys in the lock. It didn't fit. She nearly turned away, but something made her try once more with the last key. It went in and the click when she turned it felt so loud, she jumped in alarm. She slowly opened the door, just a fraction, and peered through the crack. There were descending stairs ahead and she could see a faint glimmer of light. She opened the door fully and started to go down. "Why am I doing this?" she whispered to herself, but she kept moving. Every step felt full of dread. "Go back, go back," the voice inside her said, but something else kept her going further.

As Sarah descended, the light improved, and finally she reached the bottom of the stairs. Her eyes adjusted to the gloomy light, and she cautiously looked around. She was in a very large room, full of complicated-looking machinery and strange contraptions, looking eerily menacing in the low light. At the back of the room the feeble light was moving around, then suddenly it shone straight at her. A man's voice filled the silence. "Who on earth are you?"

Chapter VII
Surviving the Gorgon

Tom woke gradually, stretching, and for a fleeting moment experiencing a feeling of wellbeing, despite his body aching from his hard work the previous day. As he lay there he wondered about where he was. Morwyn had refused to engage in a conversation about how they came to be there, and it annoyed him that there didn't appear to be a rational explanation. Sarah had seemed to be more accepting, though she still thought she might be in some sort of 'awake dream' that she'd imagined into being. He wasn't so good with things that weren't real, but he'd learnt when Gerald was punishing him that it helped to go into his imagination to stop thinking bad thoughts, and sometimes when it was really bad and he was being hit, he'd learned he could kind of escape his body so that he was watching from afar and it didn't hurt so much. Those experiences didn't come close to describing what was happening now, though. He felt annoyed and frustrated that there weren't any answers. Actually, he was more than annoyed with Morwyn — he was furious with her — for drugging him and making him feel so awful and sick, for making Sarah go on such a risky quest and now for keeping him captive. He found himself wide awake, lying there with clenched fists, and a feeling of dread and anticipation. How was he going to pretend to escape in a way that seemed real but didn't get him hurt? When would he do it? He didn't doubt that Morwyn could be forceful and violent if she got mad, and he'd seen how incredibly strong she was.

He sat up and put his pillow behind his head so he could think better. As he unclenched his fists, he saw with surprise that his hands had healed. Not only had the red gone, but the blisters had completely disappeared. How amazing! It was as if this world was challenging him to let go of his need to explain things. How else would he survive without his mind driving him mad? Part of him also wanted to believe that Hermione was special, and in particular, special to him. He got a warm feeling in his chest even thinking about her.

So, today was going to be a sieving clay day. How long did it take to dry? He was sure the stuff he was digging up yesterday wouldn't be dry in a day, but maybe Morwyn had some stored already dry. Or maybe it didn't need to be dry to sieve — why would it, when he was sure it was sieved with water? Anyway, he supposed he would have to lug it back to the stream and do it there, so he'd have to plan his escape based on where he was yesterday. She'd said that if he moved more than twenty paces she'd know, but surely that was just a ruse to keep him in one place; she couldn't magically know! What if he worked for a couple of hours, then just walked upstream and saw what happened? If he was really going to escape, he'd probably plan to do it when he'd just had food, although, at the same time, he'd also be looking out for the best opportunity whenever it appeared. Tom really wished he could talk to Sarah. He was missing her and hoped she was safe.

He got up and made his way through Morwyn's empty room to the bathroom. Did she ever sleep in her own bed, he wondered? He headed back to his room to get changed.

"Time to get moving," Morwyn snapped from behind him. "Your breakfast is on the table — you'll need to get a move on, you have a lot of work ahead of you."

He jumped. She'd scared him half to death and he fumed that she could have that effect on him — he wasn't going to let her bully him as Gerald had. He glared at her and carried on into his bedroom, shut the door and took his time getting dressed. When he emerged, he found her waiting for him — and there was nothing on the table...

"You took too long, so you've missed out on breakfast. Come on, get down the ladder."

What a cow! He was furious and felt manipulated, but he wasn't going to give in to whatever game she was playing.

*

Morwyn had returned in the early morning. She'd avoided driving anywhere near Dervla's house because she didn't want to risk Sarah seeing her and either being distracted, or giving her cause to wonder how she'd managed to leave poor, sick Thomas! Seeing Willard had given her a frisson of excitement — not just his physical presence, but more the anticipation of how she was going to trick him. And everyone said it was men who couldn't be trusted! She'd made an excuse not to see him the coming evening — there was no way she wanted to be around when he discovered the container was missing. He'd be bound to guess that she'd betrayed him somehow, and she'd rather avoid his anger. If Sarah didn't succeed, she didn't want to be linked to her and would deny all knowledge of her. She was so angry that her powers of second sight were waning. In the past she would have had a good idea of what was going to happen, but since she 'saw' that Sarah and Thomas were arriving, it hadn't been very responsive. The best chance was when she was doing something rhythmic, like her pottery, and she could let her mind wander — it seemed to coalesce into a 'knowing', but she hadn't had the chance to do that. Thomas was too present and made it impossible for her to focus in that way. Feeling increasingly panicky, Morwyn knew it was imperative to get the elixir — she would soon start to lose her strength as well. What would she be just as an aging woman and nothing special? It didn't bear thinking about.

Her anxiety fed a desire to taunt Thomas. It was like playing a game of cat and mouse. He was so gullible and predictable with his liking for the girl. If he was going to try to escape it would probably be today, and she'd be watching out for him. In the meantime, she'd have a bit of fun.

*

It turned out his task was to take dried clay (she'd stock-piled it in the kiln), pile it on a round sieve over a bucket and flush water through it, while shaking the sieve. Any impurities were left in the sieve and the fine clay went through to the bucket. It was called slaking, and it was repetitive and boring. It was also a job he could have done with the water supply up by the treehouse, but he guessed she just wanted to make him work twice as hard and suffer, having to continuously get fresh water by dipping a container into the stream. He asked why the clay had to be dry first and Morwyn curtly responded that wet clay didn't break down the same way because it resisted the penetration of water, and not to complain, as the alternative was to pulverise the dry clay and manually remove the impurities, which was much harder work.

He worked hard for about an hour. It was a tedious job that demanded his concentration, and his back was aching from having to work bent over. He stood up and stretched, hearing his stomach rumble. He'd had a good long drink from the river, but he was starving. He bet Morwyn wouldn't give him anything to eat until the evening, so why not try to make a break for it? If she was actually watching him from somewhere she must be getting pretty bored by now!

He decided to head upstream, wandering slowly at first so he could pretend he was just taking a break if Morwyn was nearby. He passed the place where he'd found the bone and shuddered and continued on, sloshing through the shallow water where it ran over river stones, and walking along the bank where it ran deeper. Soon, he was having to duck his head under trees that sent low branches out over the river, with fine foliage cascading down to touch the water a bit like the willows from home. The air was warm and sweet; heavy with scent wafting from a plant with lilac flowers, and cut through with the sound of bees lazily winding their way from flower to flower. He was tempted to sit on the bank, lean back, shut his eyes and be lulled to sleep by the sound of the water gurgling over stones — he felt a soporific pull, but resisted — he didn't have long before Morwyn would realise he was missing and she wouldn't take an attempt to escape seriously if he was happily asleep on the bank!

He kept walking up the river, though his feet were dragging and he found it really hard to take the pretence of escape seriously. He saw a curve in the river up ahead — the water looked quite deep and it was cutting into the bank, so he clambered back up onto the grass, intending to cut off the curve by walking over the top. Something caught his eye though — a smudge of brown on the face of the bank with a different texture to the clay; a smear of white near it. Neither seemed like the natural landscape, so he walked over the grassy bank and stretched out on his stomach to look at the raw face of clay below. He could see that whatever he was looking at had a smooth surface. He picked up a stick and poked at it. A bit of mud flaked off, revealing something pale underneath. He kept poking at it and realised with a fright that he'd found more bones. The brown piece he'd seen was flat, and once the mud was scraped off it looked like it might be a skull bone, while the white streak he'd seen looked like a long bone of some sort. He felt sick. Looking at the grass he was lying on, he would never have known there was a body underneath, but it had obviously been buried there and over time the river had whittled away at the bank until the bones were exposed. He imagined that's how the bone he'd found earlier had come to be downstream.

Suddenly, his light-hearted approach to running away, as a game to play against Morwyn, took on different proportions. A serious feeling of threat overtook him and left him feeling shaky and scared. Reluctantly, he got to his feet, dragging them behind him as he continued up the stream's edge. As he walked, his anxiety made his mind start to play its old tricks on him, giving way to the hated doubts and fears of his childhood. He replayed Gerald's voice telling him over and over that he was useless, and wallowed in a memory from school where he was singled out by the other boys in his class after he got the top prize, and was taken down behind the swimming pool and told he was pathetic — he knew that they were jealous of him and acting the way bullies do, but how come people thought like they could be like that with him? Maybe he really was pathetic. Maybe he should have stayed at home and taken his punishment from Gerald. If he was pathetic, he deserved it. Maybe Gerald was just trying to toughen him up. Why else would his mother take his side and not stand up for him?

Sometimes he hated himself, so much that he was scared to be seen. Or was it that he wasn't seen or wanted, so he didn't feel he had a place in the world where he could feel okay? He'd often fantasised about running away. Maybe finding himself here as Morwyn's pawn was what he'd wished for, since unhappiness was all he could trust in. How could he have fooled himself into thinking he could care for Sarah and that she'd like him back? He always ended up alone. With these dark thoughts swirling through his head, he'd stepped across a fallen tree branch before he realised that everything around him had gone eerily quiet. It suddenly felt as if the air was holding its breath, still, expectant and threatening. Tom stopped and checked around him, but even then, he was caught unprepared. One minute he was standing near the branch, the next he was lying flat on his back with all the air sucked out of his lungs. He was flattened and shocked — an evil looking, enormous creature was looming over him, its face full of hatred. It took him a while to grasp the fact that it looked like an enlarged version of the gargoyle face, he'd seen on Morwyn. Scary, twisted and vile. With a roar she snatched him up, pinning him under an arm as if he was a piece of rubbish, and strode back through the trees in the direction of the treehouse.

When they got back, Morwyn carried him up the ladder and dumped him in his room, slamming the door. He could hear her wedging something against it on the other side. He flung himself on the bed, feeling helpless and small. Even though it was only the middle of the afternoon, he was emotionally exhausted and eventually dropped into a ragged sleep.

When he woke, he sensed that it was late afternoon. He felt slightly calmer and got up to try the door. It was wedged tightly shut. He rattled the handle, with no response. He was starving and thirsty — he hadn't eaten since the previous evening. The window in his room didn't open, so he was really trapped. Anger welled up in him, raw and violent. He let it flow through him — it was so much more empowering than helplessness. He yelled and banged on the door. Nothing. In a fury, he picked up the chair and threw it at the window, flinging glass outwards in hundreds of jagged shards. He knew he couldn't escape, but it vented his energy so that he could find his mind again.

As he fell back on the bed, feeling totally spent, Hermione appeared through the broken window.

"Hermione!" He picked her up and gave her a big hug. All his self-hatred and despair and longing were wrapped up together around her soft body.

"Take heart — we'll find a way through this."

"But I'm such a coward. I thought I could stand up to her but I can't! I'm weak and no use to anyone!" he sobbed into her fur.

"That's what bullies want you to believe. The truth is that you've been hurt so much since you were very small that you can't trust yourself, let alone other people."

He put her down to concentrate more on what she was saying.

"I can't stay now. Morwyn is in the house and could come in at any time. You have a good heart. Be kind to yourself, be strong and trust that I'm here to look out for you." Hermione melted away back out the window into the tree. Only after she'd gone did he suddenly realise that she'd talked to him. He'd understood her and spoken back. He felt a sense of wonder that raised his spirits. Sarah had said something about Hermione talking to her, but he hadn't paid attention — it wasn't something he could believe in, because it was outside his experience. Now, he felt as if it was he, who had been young and silly, not Sarah. How many other things had he been closed to, he wondered? So, he *was* special to Hermione — and to Sarah. He'd had to be in absolute despair before he could listen to his feelings. The thought made him more alive somehow. It was as if something icy in his heart was starting to melt.

*

Morwyn heard the crash of breaking glass from where she was in the living room, but didn't react. The boy couldn't escape and she could hardly move. She'd used the last of her diminishing powers to enlarge and contort herself to frighten him, then carry him back. What a fool he was to think he could get away from her, yet she was now exhausted and weak, and needed to recover as much as she was able to before confronting him again. She didn't want him to sense her weakness. She'd brewed a strengthening concoction with a sedative to help her to sleep, hoping she'd wake up revitalised. Her bedroom felt too close to him, so she lay on the couch, pulling a blanket over her, sinking into a deep sleep.

*

Tom spent a fitful night, mostly in the zone half-way between awake and sleep. His dreams were repetitive and short — all about running away from something threatening that was going to kill him. Each time he woke he felt relief that it was only a dream and it was over, only to sink back into another one in a different setting but with the same feeling of threat. He woke properly at dawn, desperate to use the bathroom, but the door was still wedged shut. The only option was to pee out the window — he only hoped the Gargoyle, as he now thought of Morwyn, would be out for an early morning walk beneath his room! As he lay back down on his bed thinking of gargoyles, he remembered a story Leah had read to him when he was younger. It was a myth about the Gorgon, a woman whose hair was made of writhing snakes. If anyone looked directly at her they were turned to stone. Maybe if he didn't actually look at Morwyn she wouldn't be so scary... She certainly had something Gorgonish and evil about her. Wow, now he was sounding like Sarah.

Leah. Suddenly she was present in his mind. He'd managed to avoid thinking about her until now — somehow, he'd lumped her in with his mum and Gerald as 'That Which Is Not To Be Thought About'. Poor Leah, still stuck there. Gerald wasn't violent with her, but he knew she kept her head down to avoid his anger. And one night, when he'd got up to use the bathroom, he was sure he'd seen Gerald coming out of her room, closing the door behind him. He'd pretended to himself he hadn't seen anything and pushed the memory away, but now he felt sick thinking about what that might have meant. He couldn't help feeling as if he was back there, with his heart beating wildly, his hands and teeth clenched, as he fought a huge wave of rage that welled up on both his and Leah's behalf. He didn't think he'd feel so helpless if he saw Gerald now, even though he still got anxious just thinking about him. He was more worried now about what he'd want to do to him. And his mother — he realised that tears were leaking out of the corners of his eyes. He was partly sorry for her, ending up with a bully, but at the same time, she hadn't protected them. The disappointment actually hurt more than Gerald's violence. All they'd wanted was a kind mum, but she'd abandoned them to keep the peace.

As he turned over onto his side, facing the window, he registered that it was a bit cooler this morning. So far it had been consistently warm and fine, but it felt like the weather was turning. The leaves were rustling in a stronger breeze, and he could see dense cotton-wool clouds bunching together and chasing each other across the pale sky.

He must have dozed again, and woke to the sound of furniture scraping on the floor as whatever was wedging the door was pulled away. He braced himself as the door opened to a curt, "You've got ten minutes if you want breakfast today." He got to his feet and quickly pulled on his clothes. He gave a couple of shirts a cursory sniff before choosing one — it must be five or six days now that they'd been here — the shirts weren't too bad but he'd have to wash out his underwear later. Morwyn hadn't given them any spares. A quick trip to the bathroom, a once-over of his teeth, and he was in the living room looking at a mug of tea and toast. No adornments, just toast and butter, but it smelt wonderful. He sat down and started eating ravenously. He sniffed the mug of tea, wary from his past experiences, and put it back on the table, slowly and deliberately, getting up to fetch himself a glass of water under Morwyn's smouldering gaze. He practised not looking directly at her, and it seemed to help his nerves — hopefully she would just think he was cowed.

"Well, aren't you quiet today," she taunted. "Aren't you going to thank me for letting you have breakfast after your bad behaviour yesterday?"

Tom remained silent. Morwyn whacked her hand down hard on the table, making the plates, mugs and Tom jump.

"Look at me — I'm talking to you!"

Tom slid a glance towards her, avoiding her eyes. She was sounding angry, but he had the impression she was just playing with him, like a cat with a mouse. Well, this mouse wasn't going to lose the game, though he didn't want to antagonise her too much — surely Sarah *must* be back soon!

"What do you want from me? You can't leave me locked

up forever. Why don't you just let me go and save yourself from having to keep an eye on me?"

"I've got plans for you — and, in the meantime, I've got plenty you can do for me around here."

When they made their way down to ground level, Morwyn told him that he would have to complete the work he hadn't finished yesterday. She went to the tool cupboard at the end of the shed and pulled out a long length of chain that had a ring attached to one end of it. She placed the ring around his ankle and clicked it shut. The other end she attached to a big iron staple on the side of the shed with a padlock.

"You'll be working here today with my water supply — I can't risk you trying your disappearing trick up the river again and I don't have time to watch you all morning. If you do a decent job, I'll unchain you in the middle of the day and give you a break."

She'd obviously fetched the bucket, sieve and clay from the river sometime before breakfast, and she now pulled them out from behind the shed and plonked them down near the water pump. He spent the morning laboriously working through the lumps of clay. Mid-morning, Morwyn went off somewhere in her car, so Tom made the most of the opportunity to sit down for a while and have some water. As he'd noticed earlier, the weather was changing rapidly and the sky was now completely grey, and the wind was rising. Branches of the trees were beginning to sway, rather than just the leaves, and the temperature had dropped, which suited him since he was having to work so hard that he was sweating. He lay down for a while to think. Maybe it was something about the trees above him, but he didn't feel so bad today — he felt as if he had the strength to wait out whatever was in store for him, though the change in weather felt a bit ominous. Suddenly, from behind the shed, Hermione appeared. She sauntered over to him and rubbed her head against his shoulder. He stroked her and felt even more calm, a far cry from being so tired and nervous and upset the day before — he was beginning to realise how good it was to know someone (something?) was looking out for him. She told him it wouldn't be long now; Sarah was returning soon and they'd have to be prepared and keep their wits about them. With that, she disappeared again from wherever she'd come, as if he'd dreamt her. He pulled himself to his feet and continued with his task.

Around midday he heard the wheels of Morwyn's car scrunching on the gravel. The car swung into the clearing and stopped. Morwyn emerged from the driver's door and walked around to the passenger side of the car. She seemed to have changed her clothes — she was wearing a long, grey skirt shot with vertical, brightly coloured stripes; a pale grey shirt and a black waistcoat, closely fitting like a bodice. He hadn't been paying much attention in the morning, but he was sure she had spruced herself up for something, or someone? She opened the back passenger door and pulled out a box and a bag — he could see apples perched in the neck of the bag. As she stepped away from the car, an apple fell out of the bag and rolled onto the ground. He wasn't sure whether she tripped on the apple, or the bottom of her skirt — whichever, one minute she was standing, the next she was sprawled inelegantly, face down on the ground, and the things she was carrying went flying. He automatically went to go over and help her, but the chain on his leg pulled him up short some distance away from her, so he could only stand and watch how it played out.

She roared! She was incredibly angry. As she tried to pick herself up, she screamed at him, "Don't just stand there looking, you useless boy, come and help me!"

"I can't — you've chained me."

She swore — he almost admired the range of curses she came up with — and picked herself up, dusting down her skirt. Her black waistcoat was smeared with yellow and he realised that the box must have been filled with eggs. He saw that her hands seemed to be shaking. He didn't want to think about her maybe being vulnerable — he didn't want to start seeing her human side now and feel sorry for her!

Morwyn went up to the treehouse and emerged half an hour later, having changed her clothes. He thought she looked pale and drawn as she came over to where he'd just finished sieving the clay. She'd brought with her some tea and a sandwich, so he washed the last of the mud off his hands and sat down to eat. He pointedly tipped out the tea and refilled the mug with water, not looking to see her reaction. She told him that she was going to be spending some time clearing out her kiln so she could do another firing, and because she could keep an eye on him, she would take off his chain. She wanted him to spend the afternoon replacing one of the wooden surrounds to her raised vegetable garden, and cutting stakes for the beans. She unlocked the metal ring around his leg and showed him the rotting wood on the edge of the garden that fell in the shadow of the treehouse. There were large planks of heavy, pre-cut timber stacked around the back of the shed, that had to be lugged over to the garden and nailed into place without dislodging too much of the soil. A long afternoon stretched out ahead of him, but it was a task he could problem-solve, and he could get lost in physical work for a while, so he set himself to it with some enthusiasm. He doubted he'd get to finish it anyway — a storm was obviously approaching — the wind was now whipping around them and dark clouds were gathering.

Chapter VIII
How Much More?

"Who are you?" the voice repeated.

Sarah turned to run back up the stairs, but hesitated. There was something in the man's voice. She stopped, and slowly turned back towards him. She could now see him a little more clearly. He had a light on a strap around his head that was shining straight at her, so she could only see his shape and the angular planes of his face — and he looked as shocked to see her as she was to see him.

"I... I'm..." Sarah couldn't speak. Her mouth was suddenly dry and her tongue wouldn't go where she wanted it to.

"Don't be afraid," said the man. He moved his light away from her eyes and came slowly towards her, moving round the machinery. Up close he had a kind face and was wearing a workman's apron pulled tightly around the dungarees that clad his stocky body. She thought he seemed to be anxious too, or maybe just surprised.

"What's your name?" he asked, gently.

"Oh..." she stuttered, "I'm Sarah... wh-who are you?"

"Hello, Sarah, I'm Arthur," he replied. "Willard has kept us prisoner down here."

"Why...? What for...?" Sarah couldn't quite believe what she was seeing. "How long have you been here?" she finally asked.

"We're not sure because there's no window to let in daylight and we've lost track of the days, but I think it's been a few weeks."

"Who else is here with you?"

"My wife, Mary, is locked in a cage at the back of the room. Willard makes me work for him and if I refuse, he won't give her any food."

Sarah suddenly thought about the other key on Willard's chain. "I've got his key ring and I haven't found out yet what one of the keys is for. Let's try it," she said, suddenly feeling more confident, and keen to help. Arthur led her to the back of the room.

"Mind the machinery," he said, as they wove their way around metal pipes, and gears and wheels.

At the very back of the room, in a dark corner, Sarah could just make out a large cage with iron bars from floor to ceiling. Inside was a woman in a rather grubby yellow dress with her hair pulled back from her face, looking tired and scared. She put the key in the lock, and it turned. The door opened, and Mary ran out into her husband's arms.

"It's okay, Mary. This is Sarah — we're going to get out of here!"

"We need to go as quickly as we can," Sarah said, keeping her voice down. "I've given Willard a sleeping draught, but I'm not sure how long it will last for."

Mary gathered up some papers from one of the tables and they started up the stairs. Half way up, Arthur stopped. "Hold on a minute, I'll be right with you." He went back down, picked up a hammer and smashed it repetitively into a contraption sitting on the work bench. Sarah couldn't tell what it was. He'd clearly destroyed it, but she was petrified that the noise would wake Willard, so she was relieved when he dropped the hammer and followed them back up the stairs, the light on his head helping them to see the way.

At the top, Sarah closed the door and locked it, whispering, "It might buy you a bit of time if he doesn't think to look down there for a while." They walked quickly down the corridor, past the still sleeping Willard and out the front door.

"We need to talk somewhere," Mary said.

"I know where we can go — follow me." Sarah led the way quickly back along Cross Street, checking that Ryder was following them. When they got to the town square she skirted around the edge of the market and back to where she'd left the bike. The market was now very busy, with clusters of people standing around the stalls and talking in groups in the square. There was a buzz and bustle to the place that, ordinarily, Sarah would like to have lingered over. Instead, she turned to the couple, just as Ryder gently sank down from a tree and landed on her shoulder.

"This is my friend, Ryder," said Sarah.

Arthur stepped forward and offered his hand for Ryder to nibble. "He's a wonderful specimen. Ryder, Sarah, can I introduce us properly to you? I'm Arthur Birch and this is my wife, Mary. We'd like to thank you from the bottom of our hearts for rescuing us from that place."

"You're very welcome…"

"We've got a lot to talk about — how about you go first

with how you came to be at Willard's house," said Mary.

"Actually, I'm dying to know — please tell me how you ended up in Willard's basement?"

"Arthur, why don't you go over to Gerand's stall and get us some food — he'll be happy to let us pay later and I bet he's been worried about where on earth we've been. I'll start telling Sarah what's happened."

"Ryder, can you keep an eye out for Willard to make sure he doesn't come to the square while we're talking?" Ryder launched himself off Sarah's shoulder and flew up to a tree near the entrance to Cross Street, where he also had a good view of the other streets leading to the square.

"Clever bird!" Arthur remarked as he walked away to the stall.

Sarah and Mary sat down on the bench. She was a bit rounded, like her husband, and not much taller than Sarah. She pulled her curly brown hair out of its clasps, shaking it loose to her shoulders with a big sigh. She had blue eyes that crinkled in the corners when she smiled, which Sarah found comforting — she just knew that Mary was kind. She guessed that she was somewhere in her mid-forties, not that numbers that big meant a lot to her — she wasn't much good at telling age, but she was probably a similar age to her parents.

"Well," Mary began, "Arthur and I live at Riverstone, a mill over to the west."

"Oh, I've been there, I think," interrupted Sarah. "I was there a few days ago and it was deserted."

"Yes, I guess it would have seemed like that. We moved into the mill a couple of years ago, and it really was deserted then. It hadn't been a working mill for years, but both Arthur and I are engineers — Arthur is the practical one who can make anything work, and I'm more of a designer — a sort of an idea's person — between us we make a very good team, and we soon got it working again. Anyway, about four weeks ago, early one evening, we were sitting talking when there was a knock on the door. Arthur answered it and Willard was standing there. We didn't know him personally, but we'd heard a bit about him and he certainly seemed to know all about us! As soon as he was inside the house, he pulled out a knife and grabbed me, holding the knife to my throat. I've never been so scared!" Mary paused and took a deep breath. "He made Arthur go outside and dragged me out with him. He had a car and he forced Arthur into the front passenger seat and made me get in the back with him. He still held the knife against me and threatened to use it if we didn't do what he said. It was awful! The person sitting in the driving seat was a woman called Morwyn, who lives on the way to Hunterdale."

"We know her!" exclaimed Sarah, "In fact, she's the reason I'm here now. She's a terrible person, but I guess if it wasn't for her I wouldn't have found you." Sarah looked at Mary with a tentative smile.

"Well, let's be thankful for that," replied Mary, looking back at Sarah with a smile of her own. "Anyway, once we were all in the car, Morwyn drove us to Hunterdale, and Willard forced us into his basement and we've been there ever since."

"But what did he want you for?"

"Willard must have heard about what we did to restore the mill and get it going, and he wanted to use our skills to work for him. He's been trying to build some sort of flying machine to take him up Greyvyn — that's a volcanic mountain south of here. Both he and Morwyn seem to be completely obsessed with the need to get there, but we don't know for sure what for. We think that it's something to do with rumours about flowers that grow up there, but who knows if there's any truth in that."

"I think I know — there's some sort of special honey that the bees on Greyvyn make from narcissus flowers, and Morwyn wants me to try to get it, and she's kept my friend, Tom, captive to make sure I do. Adults can't climb the mountain because they're too big and heavy for the narrow path, so Morwyn's making me go because I'm much smaller. I don't think she trusts Willard, and she wants the honey for herself — it's supposed to prolong life."

"Well, this is all starting to make some sort of sense. With a flying machine he could bypass the path," said Mary, nodding to herself as she put Sarah's story together with her own. "Be very careful — whether it's true or not, folklore around here says that half way up Greyvyn there's a magical bridge spanning a chasm that a seeker has to pass over to get to the top, and that only someone light — I guess that means young — and pure of heart can cross it. Anyone else will be stricken with an illness that causes premature aging and death. So, while what Morwyn said is true about the narrow and dangerous path, people are more afraid of the bridge — there's no way of crossing it without risking death."

"Oh, my goodness, that's awful. What if it's true? Who on earth is 'pure of heart'?" Sarah started to feel panicky and it came out in her shaky voice.

"Please don't worry, Sarah. It may not even be true, and if anyone is pure of heart it would be someone like you. I imagine it's just a story to keep people away... Anyway, to finish off our part in all this — we started off pretending to work for him with no intention of making something that would actually fly — it seemed to be all the better if he crashed," she continued, "But then he stuck me in that cage and wouldn't feed me unless Arthur made visible progress every day on the flying machine. He also made it clear that if he didn't come back from the flight, Morwyn would 'dispose' of us, so Arthur just had to start making it properly."

At this point, Arthur returned with something hot and steaming wrapped in paper — it smelt so good that Sarah's mouth started watering, and for a few minutes they ate in silence. Sarah then told them both her understanding of what had happened over the last few days, starting with her and Tom's strange entrances into this world, their confusion and the things that happened since. She finished by describing her experiences of the last two days, and finding the container, and then the two of them in Willard's house. Mary put her arm around her shoulders and squeezed them. Sarah's eyes filled with tears — it was much harder to keep strong when someone was being kind to her, but she let herself lean into her a little and accept her gesture of comfort.

Arthur leaned towards her and patted her knee. "Are you sure you need to carry on with Morwyn's plan, Sarah? Perhaps we could go back to Riverdale together and then see how we could rescue Tom... If you have to go, we wish we could come with you, but we can't climb Greyvyn, and I think we'd be best to get back to Riverstone and make sure we secure it in case Willard returns for us. I doubt he will, once he realises he's lost the container, but he's a nasty piece of work and we're going to have to keep our wits about us."

"And we can't go to Morwyn's for Tom either," joined in Mary, "Because she's made sure no one can get into the treehouse unless she lets them. We obviously can't turn up and ask her to let us in, since we're supposed to be safely locked away at Willard's."

"This land, called North Feasgar, is fairly benign and peaceful, but inevitably, there will always be people who exploit others for their own use — Morwyn and Willard are well suited in that regard!" Arthur scratched his head and grimaced, as if he couldn't believe how people could be so entirely out for themselves. He had a nice face too; a bit craggy, with hazel eyes and greying hair that stood up in a peak over his forehead. "We'll walk back with you to the bridge, but if you're going to carry on with Morwyn's plan, then you'll have to follow Landing Road along the river to the jetty. Mary, why don't you give Sarah your cardigan so she doesn't get too sunburnt on the water — you won't need it today since it's so warm?" Sarah looked down at her skin. It was fair, but she tanned easily. It was darkening up already from being outdoors for the last couple of days, but she might not find shelter again for a while, so she took the cardigan gratefully.

The three of them made their way together back along Market Road to the bridge. Mary wrapped her arms around Sarah, giving her a hug.

"Go well, Sarah. You're a brave girl. Remember that, whatever happens next. When you come back, we'll be at Riverstone waiting for you and Tom. My regret is that you have to do the next part on your own."

"Well, not really on my own — I have Ryder." Sarah looked up to check and, sure enough, there he was, circling in the sky, keeping an eye out for any signs of danger. Arthur also enfolded Sarah in a big embrace, slipping something round and flat into her hand.

"That's for good luck and to remind you we're here for you, any time."

They walked off quickly to the bridge, leaving Sarah standing alone, holding back tears. She wiped her eyes and looked down at her hand, where she saw a coin that looked familiar, with the Queen's head on it. She turned it over — it had £1 stamped on it, and the year 1987. Where would he have got it from? She stared after him, and as if he felt her eyes burning into his back, he turned and gave her a strange half salute before walking on with his wife.

*

Sarah reluctantly started off down Landing Road, following the River Dearth to where the riverboat was moored. It was a pleasant walk and she let herself be comforted by the sounds of the river and of people going about their daily business. She'd panicked earlier getting out of Willard's house, thinking he may wake up, but with distance she could think more clearly and remembered that Tom's first draught left him sleeping for several hours, and even though Willard was an adult, she'd added to the dose to make up for that. She still had thirty minutes to get to the riverboat by one o'clock, and her nerves needed a rest. As she wandered, she thought about Mary and Arthur. They hadn't been at all fazed when she told them how she'd got to their world, and then Arthur had given her the coin, obviously from Britain. Maybe they'd met people before who'd come through the rift as she and Tom had?

She looked up to see a jetty about fifty yards away. A boat was moored on its downriver side, a couple of smaller vessels on the side upriver, and pulled up on the river bank before the jetty there was a cluster of canoes. As she got closer, she could see a few people milling around the riverboat mooring, talking animatedly and gesticulating. One man, looking angry, was waving his fist at another, who raised both hands in the air is if to say, 'I can't do anything about it' and stepped back from the jetty onto the boat. As Sarah stepped onto the jetty the group of people came back towards her. A woman said, "No boat today, there's an engine problem," as she walked past her. Sarah hurried on down the jetty to the boat, panic starting to rise again. She called out to the man on the boat, "Hello, hello? Is there something wrong with the boat? When will it be fixed? I have to get to Greyvyn today."

"Sorry, miss, nothing I can do. Her engine's dead and I don't know how long it will take to fix. I'm sure she'll be running again in the morning."

"But I have to get there today," she said in distress.

"Your only option is to hire a canoe, if you know how to use one." He turned his back to her and disappeared through a hatch into the engine room.

Completely dispirited, she walked back along the jetty, checking the smaller boats on the other side as she went. She knew she'd never be able to afford to hire one, but in any case, they were deserted. Back at the road she stepped off the shoulder onto the grass verge, making her way down the slope to where a man was sitting near the canoes, whittling a long piece of wood with a knife. As she approached, he turned to look at her. His skin was dark and weathered, as if he'd spent a lifetime outdoors. He had a furrow between his brows and the corners of his dark eyes were creased from squinting into the sun.

"How much would it cost me to hire one of your canoes to get me to Greyvyn? I only have enough money for the return fare on the river boat, but it isn't running today."

"The return fare will cover it," his voice gruff and gravelly.

"But how will I get back again if I give it all to you?" Sarah asked uncertainly.

"Not my problem. You don't look like you'd be strong enough to paddle back upriver, but you can leave the canoe at the Greyvyn jetty and the captain of the river boat will put it on board and return it to me."

Sarah sat down on the slope to think. She realised she really didn't have a choice — she had to get to Greyvyn today before Willard followed her. She'd just have to do it and worry about how on earth she'd get back later. She could probably walk or hitch a lift if she had to — Arthur had said it was about twice the distance it was from the treehouse to Hunterdale, so it was manageable even though it felt like the last thing she would want to do — she was already worn out with all her worrying.

"Well... do you want it or not?"

"Yes, please. Can you show me the best way of paddling it? I've been in one a little bit like it before, but not the same." The kayaks she'd tried at home had been made of something like hard plastic — these looked more solid. She couldn't tell what they were made from — probably wood, because here was a wooden seat across the middle for her to sit on. And the top was open, whereas she was used to sitting in a moulded seat further down inside it. There was a dual ended paddle though, not the single ones that went with the canoes she'd seen on TV. The man pulled one of the smaller canoes towards the river and chose a paddle with a short span. He also pulled out something bulky and green from a pile, which turned out to be a life jacket — the outer material was tough and looked like canvas. She couldn't tell what was inside it, but when he gave it to her to put on, it was much heavier than what she was used to. She made sure that the casket, now containing the gold thread, was carefully rolled inside the waist band of her tights. She pulled her top and Mary's cardigan down over it, and then put the life jacket over her head and tied the tapes securely on either side, following the man down to the river's edge where he was holding one end of the canoe, while the other was swinging gently in the pull of the water.

He held the canoe steady as she clambered in. It felt strange sitting on the seat — oddly high up compared to what she was used to. He handed her the paddle and showed her how to rotate her shoulders to dip the correct edge into the water on either side. It wasn't that difficult, since it was the type of paddle she was used to — she was very glad that it wasn't a single one.

"Keep to the centre of the river. The current is swift there, but deeper, so you won't get into trouble with the rocks. The edges can be treacherous, especially where the river curves, and you won't want to be caught in the rapids there."

Sarah thanked him, took a deep breath and manoeuvred her canoe slowly out from the bank towards the jetty. At first, the canoe responded to her sluggishly, and she spent a bit of time getting used to steering it before heading out towards the centre of the river to get past the jetty. There, the current picked up and she began gliding along at an alarming rate. Her heart was pounding, partly exhilarated, partly in terror, and she had to focus really hard on keeping up a steady rhythm so the canoe didn't wobble, while rapidly speeding away from Hunterdale.

Sarah successfully navigated down a straight piece of river and around a bend. She noticed that she had to correct the canoe to make sure the current didn't push her too far towards the bank on the outside of the bends, but overall, it didn't seem too hard. She didn't need to use much energy paddling, as the current carried the canoe along effortlessly. So far, the river seemed to have straight stretches, punctuated by curves that cancelled each other out so that she was being pulled constantly towards the south. After about fifteen minutes though, the terrain either side started to look rockier. The river narrowed between rocky outcrops jutting into the water either side of the river like jagged teeth. At the same time the river became windier, and she had to concentrate to safely navigate around them, constantly correcting so the canoe didn't take her into the side of a bend.

She was starting to feel tired, not from exertion, but from the emotional pressure of concentrating. Her dad had always told her that the best sportspeople did well, not because of their strength, but because they had nerves of steel. Well, hers weren't steel — she could feel them vibrating like the plucked string of an instrument, maybe one with high notes like a screechy violin. They were jangling and exhausting! Oops, her mind had wandered and she found herself over-correcting as she turned a fraction too late through a bend. The canoe wobbled and she was suddenly juddering and twisting across some mini-rapids at the side of the river near the bank. She was then pitched straight into the next bend before she'd managed to straighten up, and the canoe bucked across the current. She hurtled towards the bank of the next curve sideways and she knew she wasn't going to make it. The only thing she could think to do was to try to push against the rocks on the bank with her paddle to try to keep away from them, so she lifted it with her right arm and pushed out with all her strength. The paddle jammed between two rocks and she heard a splintering sound as the end snapped off, leaving her with just one good end she could use. She was preparing to switch it to the other side of the canoe when she saw that she was now being dragged over to the left bank, still off course from the middle of the river. She couldn't correct it as she was too clumsy with just one oar.

The canoe hit the bank and suddenly she was in the water, tumbling and twisting, upside down, sideways, like a puppet being jerked by the water-master, the canoe slipping away from her and continuing on rapidly downstream. She had water up her nose, in her ears, she didn't know which way was up and she hit her left shoulder with a sickening thump on a rock. The life jacket then managed to pull her upright above water and as she gasped for air, she could see that she'd tumbled along the left bank and there were rocks coming up ahead — all she could do was reach out and grab hold of a rock as she flew by. Her shoulder was wrenched hard as the current pushed her body away from her arm around the rock. It was agonising, but she held on. After what seemed like ages, she managed to stretch her feet down against the fast-flowing current to see if they could find a purchase on the river bed. Her left foot pushed against some stones, just enough that she could start to inch her way around the rock into the calmer lee of the other side. Sarah clambered soggily over the stones and up onto the bank, pitching head first onto the ground, chest heaving and with her injured shoulder sending shafts of pain down her arm and up towards her neck. She lay there for about ten minutes, shaking with shock, until gradually her heavy breathing subsided and the pain in her shoulder settled into a grinding ache. She rolled over and sat up. There was no sign of the canoe. She presumed it would find its own way down to the Greyvyn jetty — maybe someone would think to rescue it there. There was nothing she could do about it!

She untied the tapes at the side of her life jacket and pulled it over her head, wincing as another streak of fire tore down her left arm. She took off Mary's cardigan and lay down on her back, letting the sun dry off her top and tights. Her hair felt stiff and tangled, matted from catching on debris in the river on top of not being washed for a few days, but she didn't dare take it out of her ponytail or she'd probably look even more of a fright. She was lucky it was a warm day — how miserable she'd have been if she'd been wet and cold! Suddenly, she remembered with a sense of panic to check her tights for the container — it was still intact under her waistband and she sighed with relief. Thank goodness, though how she was ever going to get to Greyvyn now didn't bear thinking about. She felt completely defeated, consumed with a sense of sodden despair. She wallowed in being totally alone and helpless, until she remembered what Hermione had said about help being there when she needed it, so long as she stayed open to trust. Last time she really needed help Ryder had been there for her. So where was he now? She realised she hadn't seen him since she got to the jetty, but at the same time he hadn't agreed to stick with her, and maybe he had other things to do.

Sarah stood up gingerly on the bank. It seemed as though every part of her hurt, but her shoulder was the worst. It was much rockier here, and there were fewer trees and shrubs. She could see the mountain peak in the distance. *How am I ever going to get there?* she thought to herself again, despondently. She had no idea how far she'd travelled down the river — Tom would probably know how to work that out. No doubt he could calculate how fast the river was flowing or something. Thinking of him, stuck with Morwyn, just made her feel worse. Surely, she wouldn't keep him drugged the whole time she was away — that would be really bad for him.

Part of her just wanted to lie back down on the bank and wallow in feeling bad, but another, stronger, part of her knew she had to keep going. Spying a branch caught between two rocks on the water's edge, she pulled it out with her good arm and using it to give her support, started walking along the river bank towards the mountain.

Sarah had no sense of how long she walked or how far she travelled. She drifted into a shambling walk with her head down, just concentrating on putting one foot in front of the other. She could feel loneliness and helplessness overpowering her. All she wanted was for this to be over. Tears started to slide down her face, slowly at first, but gathering into an avalanche that thickened the back of her nose and throat, making her nose run, her eyes smart and her face feel blotchy. Exhaustion and despair finally overtook her, and she sat down heavily on the side of the path, put her head on her arms across her knees, and sobbed and sobbed and sobbed.

How long she sat there she didn't know. She drifted into an exhausted sleep. Tom, Hermione, Ryder, Mr. and Mrs. Birch, Morwyn and Willard swirled around in her mind making dreams that didn't make sense, and when she awoke it was late afternoon. She thought again about Ryder — she'd set him free and maybe he'd gone forever. But not long after, as if he'd been summoned by her thoughts, she heard a distant screech and looked up. The sun had lowered in the sky and was so bright she had to shade her eyes, but when she squinted, she could see a dark speck circling above her. Suddenly, there was Ryder, gliding effortlessly towards her on a current of air. He drifted down and landed on a rock close to her. It was enough to make her start crying again, but this time they were tears of relief — she wasn't alone any more.

"Oh, Ryder, I thought you'd gone forever. I capsized the canoe and hurt myself, and I've felt so alone and helpless. I thought I couldn't go on any further and that something terrible would happen to Tom and that it would be all my fault, and my shoulder hurts, and I thought I would never see you again and..." She stopped. Ryder sidled over to her and gently brushed his wing across her hunched shoulders.

"What am I going to do, Ryder?" she asked in a whisper, as though saying it out loud would make her helplessness too real. "I still have the container, but I just don't think I can walk any further, and I have to save Tom."

"What's the container for? You didn't tell me what you had to do after leaving Willard's…"

Sarah gave him a brief explanation of what her task up the mountain was. Just telling him about it made her breathless with fear, and when she got to the bit about having to cross the bridge with a 'pure heart' she started to cry.

"I don't even know what that means. I've been mean sometimes to my friends, I haven't always been a good kid for my parents. My dad works so hard, but I get cross that we don't do things together. What if…?"

"Stop, Sarah!" Ryder said forcefully. "You're just young; you can't know everything all at once. You have a good heart and of course you'd get across the bridge."

Sarah took a deep breath and tried to calm herself down. "But I'm so tired, and it all seems too big for me."

"So, why don't you ask for help?"

"Who from? I'm all on my own," Sarah replied despondently.

"Really?" Ryder asked.

"Oh!" she said, looking at him. "I'm sorry, of course you're here, but what can you do?"

"Well, what can I do that you can't do?"

Sarah thought for a minute, then realised how slow she'd been in her panic. "You can fly…"

"Yes, I can. So, give me the container — I'll go. I can fly there and back easily before nightfall, so long as the bee keeper is willing to give the honey to me."

"Really? Would you do that for me?" She felt overwhelmed — grateful that he was willing to go, and relieved that she didn't have to muster the courage to go up the mountain. Not just getting up the path, but also there was the horrible possibility of not getting over the bridge and maybe even dying. She stroked the feathers on the back of his head and thanked him, with tears of relief rolling down her cheeks.

Before he made to leave, she asked, "Did you see anywhere with a bit of cover where I can wait?"

"If you go back a little over there," he pointed with his beak slightly north-east, "You'll find a stand of small trees and bushes. You'll have to find some berries or something to eat. Unless you want me to bring you rabbit, that is!" He cackled with the noise she took to be laughter. "Wait for me there. If I haven't returned by tomorrow morning, you'll know something's gone wrong and you'll need to head back to Hunterdale. Don't eat any small, round black berries, they're poisonous."

"Oh, they sound like deadly nightshade. Fancy having them here as well. My grandfather warned me about them. Take care, Ryder; please return safely. And thank you!"

She gave him the container, which he gripped carefully between his talons. He launched himself slightly awkwardly into the air and flew off, soaring up higher and higher until he was just a black speck. She suddenly felt like crying again. She was alone, with no shelter or food and didn't know if everything was going to turn out all right. All she could do was trust that he would do his best. She sighed, turned in the opposite direction, and started walking back up the river and inland towards the greenery he'd pointed out to her. Near the trees she found some bushes that looked like blackberries, though they had much longer spikes protecting them than what she was used to. Reaching for them, she managed to rip some skin off her hands, but they looked plump and delicious. She gathered them into Mary's cardigan and walked on. The trees were clumped together surrounding a rocky outcrop and she manoeuvred herself into the undergrowth, finding a smooth rock to lean against that was covered on the sides and above by greenery. She settled down to wait, using the life jacket as a pillow.

*

Her mind circled, words and worries winding their way annoyingly through a half sleep as she dozed through the rest of the afternoon. So, why exactly was she going ahead with this silly plan? Why would she want to do anything to help Morwyn? Other than to save Tom of course — she couldn't let him down now, plus she'd done so much already, she didn't want it to all be for nothing. Besides, she wasn't a quitter — she always did her best — her parents said she was stubborn. She'd never experienced anything like this, though. She couldn't believe it was only this morning she'd been in Willard's house! What was she going to do if they didn't get the honey? Actually, what was she going to do if they *did* get the honey? There was no way she wanted to give it to Morwyn. What if she did something dreadful with her powers? She'd feel responsible. Could she trick her and give her something fake? She couldn't imagine Morwyn falling for a trick though — she wasn't stupid. She'd be sure to hold them there until she knew the elixir was working. Would she let them go even then? It looked like she'd have to make a plan to safeguard both her and Tom. But she was so tired. Her shoulder was aching, she'd only had berries to eat and she was still shaken from the river incident. She didn't want to have to think, and just wanted someone to tell her what to do!

Sarah was exhausted, but her thoughts wouldn't leave her alone. At one point when she dropped off into a fitful sleep, she dreamt about being chased and woke up with a start, with Willard's name hanging in the air in front of her, as if someone had said it out loud. She felt panicky, imagining maybe her thoughts would conjure him up, until she told herself she was being silly. But the idea of magical thinking remained. What if Morwyn really did know that they knew what she was up to? Maybe she could read their thoughts and was just playing with them? If Morwyn had the Sight, why couldn't she see what was going on, unless, as Hermione said, she was losing her power? It was all so convoluted — Morwyn thinking she was tricking them, them thinking they were ahead of her in her game. What did she really know; she was just a kid...?

She must have fallen properly asleep, because it was nearing dusk when she woke to the sound of cars. It sounded like there were a couple of vehicles out on the road near her, with drivers who were fooling around — it reminded her of the boy racers from the council estate near her place at home. They were yelling at each other and screeching the tyres in the gravel. One of them yelled, "Go!" and they took off, accelerating down the road with a flurry of stones. It was kind of comforting to hear people doing silly things familiar to her when she'd been feeling so isolated.

The sun had lowered to that lovely golden stage where her skin glowed and everything looked somehow more intense — a totally different quality to the light from earlier in the day. She stretched and checked herself out — her shoulder still ached, but the pain felt a bit more manageable. Pulling down the neckline of her shirt over her shoulder revealed the beginnings of a purple bruise extending from the inner part of her shoulder down the inside of her arm. That was going to look pretty in a couple of days! Sarah stood up and nearly jumped out of her skin with fright as a host of little birds nesting in the trees above her burst into life and rose into the sky, calling out their annoyance at being disturbed with shrill cries. They flew in formation in a long, lazy, double spiral up in the air and then sank down to their perches again. They reminded her of the starlings at home and were really rather beautiful — but they'd given her such a fright!

The sun was now sinking rapidly and she noticed that the sky was turning inky blue, without any hint of pink. If that meant what she was familiar with (her grandfather had always said 'Red sky at night, shepherd's delight'), maybe the fine weather was going to break tomorrow. She decided to make the most of the remaining light to go back to the river to get some water. She managed to gather a few more berries on her way, but it was hard to see the spikes and she had to abandon them when her hands started to get torn. She wished she had her phone so she could use its light, and also to know what the time was. It was funny, though, how little she missed it, when it had been so important before.

The water raced, dark and oily-looking; swirling around the rocks and flattening the reeds growing along the bank. Sarah had allowed herself to forget just how swift the current was, and she shuddered, remembering how scary her tumble out of the canoe had been. She knelt down at the water's edge and scooped up handfuls of water, gulping it down, realising how thirsty she was. She splashed some over her face and neck, longing for a good hot shower and some soap. Making her way back to her hideaway in the gathering dusk, she felt a little calmer than she had been earlier in the day. She was resigned to waiting for Ryder's return, accepting that if he wasn't there by daybreak, she would begin the journey back to the treehouse and plan what to do on her way. As she pushed herself through the undergrowth to the rocky grove, a dark shape drifted down from his lookout perch in a tree where he'd been waiting, and alighted on the ground next to her, dropping the golden container by her feet.

"Ryder! You're back! Thank goodness — it's so good to see you."

Sarah made herself comfortable as Ryder told her the story of his afternoon. He'd flown directly to Greyvyn, circling the treeline of the mountain for some time to make sure there was no danger. He didn't see any humans, though it had been tempting to hunt, as small prey seemed to thrive in the undergrowth there! He'd then flown lower, skimming the tree tops near the path until he found the beekeeper's hut. Perching on a branch directly overlooking it, he watched as the beekeeper went about his business stacking firewood. He was a little man, wiry, with long hair and a beard, wearing brightly coloured, woven clothes. Ryder knew that the few Little People left in the land could speak to birds, but he hadn't realised he'd been spotted until he said, "So what do you want,

Feathers?"

Ryder told him why he was there, and Drogal, for that was the little man's name, invited him down to where he was now sitting on the porch outside his front door. Ryder declined, though he moved down the tree to a branch a little closer. He didn't quite trust him — he had a tricky air about him and he didn't want to end up as hawk stew! They'd ended up having a long conversation — Drogal liked to talk and didn't see anyone sometimes for weeks on end. He'd told him that he'd been the beekeeper for many, many years, taking just enough of the elixir himself to keep him healthy so he could carry on as its guardian. No one had successfully ventured up the mountain for a very long time, but once a year, at the midsummer solstice, he took honey to the bottom of the mountain at night, where a man met him and paid him his annual salary in gold. He didn't ask questions, content to know that he was paid well for his guardianship of the honey, but the man had an expensive car, with a driver, probably coming from the city to the east of Hunterdale as no one in the district was that wealthy. Drogal left the mountain once a month to sell the garments and cloth that he wove, and to buy provisions and thread at the market in Hunterdale. In the months before he met the man each year, he was tasked with buying gold thread and silk to make a fine garment for him. He was paid handsomely for this on top of his salary. It turned out that the woman he bought his thread from was Dervla. Once she'd given him wine, which had loosened his tongue, and he'd told her about the elixir, which must have been how Willard had come to hear about it.

Ryder asked why he was talking so freely to him — it seemed like he'd be safer keeping the story to himself, to which Drogal had replied that he was the last of the Little People left in North Feasgar and the only person who could speak to birds. No other humans from the land could do that — those with traces of magic only had the Sight, so Ryder wouldn't have anyone to talk to about him. Ryder laughed to himself, thinking about Sarah!

Eventually, they'd got down to business. Ryder told him he wanted the golden container filled with honey in exchange for a golden thread, which he'd been told was the payment he asked for. Drogal agreed and asked him to bring them to him. As Ryder still didn't entirely trust him, he stayed on his perch, saying that he would drop the container and once it was filled with honey, which he was to do within his sight, he was to put it on a branch. He would leave the thread on the other side of Drogal and they would each pick up their payment at the same time. Drogal had laughed, saying that his ancestry was a pure line back to the most powerful, regal and respected of the Little People. This lineage might mean he could be tricky with the unwary or undeserving, but not dishonest. They agreed to do as Ryder suggested, and he left him with both gold threads rather than one. When he had the container safely out of reach, they'd carried on talking, telling stories and exchanging riddles until the sun started to dip down behind the trees, and he bid Drogal farewell. His parting words were of caution — he'd noticed some changes of late and was wondering whether there could be magical activity in the south that might be bringing trouble. He hadn't wanted to say any more, but said that Ryder would always be welcome should he have need of him.

After finishing his story, Ryder and Sarah talked quietly for a while. She had many questions that he did his best to answer.

"Thank you so, so much, Ryder. I couldn't have managed without you!"

"No, thank you for freeing me. I chose to help you today, just as I'm choosing to continue with you on your journey. To have a real choice without conditions is to be truly free. Even if I make a choice I regret later, it is still mine to make, and for that I thank you. Now that it's dark I'm going to find you some moss to put on your shoulder to reduce the swelling, then I'm going hunting for my dinner. I'm sorry, I can't help you with that!"

He flew off, returning a while later with some damp moss that Sarah packed onto her bruises. He told her he'd wake her early so she could get on the road — if she had to walk all the way to Hunterdale it was going to be a long day.

*

Sarah slept fairly well, considering the hardness of the ground and her sore shoulder, waking to the early bird chorus and then Ryder tapping her on her good shoulder. The sky was slightly pink on the horizon, casting a glow on the river that was a little unearthly. Her injured shoulder felt a bit better and she carefully cleaned the moss off it in the river. Then she had a drink and a quick wash before starting her walk towards Hunterdale. About thirty minutes later, at a point where she'd reached the weary state of trudging, a vehicle approached from the direction of Greyvyn and she turned to wave to the driver of what turned out to be a small truck with an open back. It drove past, then slowed down and stopped a little ahead of her. A middle-aged man, a bit portly, dressed in farming clothes and boots, got out and called out to her, "Do you want a lift? You'll have to get on the back with the apples 'cause the passenger seat is stacked with things for the orchard, but you're welcome to have a ride. It's a long walk to Hunterdale. I wonder what a young girl like you is doing out here alone?"

Sarah didn't know what to do. Her mother had always impressed on her the danger of talking to strangers and to never, ever, accept a ride with one. But what was a girl to do? She was tired, hungry, dirty, her hair felt matted, her shoulder ached, her clothes looked disgusting and she was stuck in some godforsaken world, who knows how far from Hunterdale, alone! She was so over it! The man seemed ordinary enough, so she decided to say yes, silently praying that if she was making a mistake, Ryder would swoop down and peck out his eyeballs!

"Oh, thank you so much. Are you going to Hunterdale then?"

"I'm passing through it. I could drop you off in Landing Road at the junction of Market Street. Would that do you?"

"Yes, please. That would be wonderful," Sarah replied, with a sense of relief that almost overpowered her. She clambered up onto the back of the truck as the man got back into the driver's seat, making a space for herself between boxes of apples. As the truck bumped down the road, quite a rough ride on the gravel, Sarah wedged herself into a sitting position with her back against the cab and her legs stretched out between the boxes. She would have thought it impossible, but she dropped off into a fitful doze. She was dreaming about a creature that was lying in wait for her. She was in a forest and couldn't see it but she could feel a menacing presence. She jerked awake as the truck went around a corner, feeling scared, her heart pounding. She'd somehow managed to slide down onto the truck deck while she was asleep and was lying, slightly turned on her side, her face pressed to the timber. From this angle she could see a bundle of ropes squashed between the boxes and something metallic. She sat up and pulled on the rope. The shiny thing moved and clinked — she realised she was seeing the links of a metal chain. What would he use ropes and chains for? Her sluggish mind slowly registered that she hadn't liked the way he'd spoken about her being a young girl alone... She started panicking. Part of her thought she was being silly, but her dream, along with her parents' warnings, overpowered her. Her chest felt tight with anxiety and her breathing was shallow and gaspy, leaving her feeling light-headed, and she forced herself to breathe deeply and look up at her surroundings.

Thank goodness — there was Hunterdale ahead — she could see the plumes of steam rising in the air. Nearly there — she could hang in a little longer. She began to calm down and was starting to think she might have been over-reacting. But as they drew near to the intersection, other than braking for other vehicles, the truck driver didn't seem to be slowing down. He drew closer to the intersection — and drove straight on through it. Sarah banged on the back of the cab, but the man didn't give any indication that he'd heard her. Getting panicky, she moved to the back of the truck and looked around her, wondering what to do. The truck wasn't moving all that fast because of other vehicles, but she would still injure herself if she jumped off. She didn't have long to decide what to do, because he could speed up again as soon as he cleared the town. She was clinging to the side of the truck, her hands sweaty and with a lump in her throat, when a dark shape came down out of the sky towards her, hovering above her for a moment — just long enough for Ryder to say, "Next corner, jump to the left onto the grass."

She looked ahead and could see a corner approaching. As the truck slowed down, she gathered herself together, bending and tucking her left arm to her chest so she could roll when she hit the ground. The truck swung into the corner, veering to the right, and Sarah took a deep breath and threw herself off the truck, hitting the grass verge with a thud on her left side, then rolling onto her back. She was winded and her shoulder screamed at her in agony. Tears were streaming down her face. Gasping, she sat up and noticed with a slap of terror that the truck was stopping up ahead.

"Hey, girl, are you all right? Did you fall off that truck?" A man ran across the road to her and knelt down beside her.

"I jumped! The man who was giving me a ride wouldn't let me get off — and I think was trying to kidnap me," she sobbed. He helped her to her feet, putting his arm around her shoulders. He looked angrily in the direction of the truck and led her across the road and into a shop.

"Here, sit down, you're as white as a sheet!" She found herself sitting in a chair behind a counter. The shop looked like it sold leather goods, with hand-made bags and shoes displayed on shelves, and leather-working tools on the bench.

"Hold on, I'll get you a glass of water."

Sarah looked towards the door, and the man, seeing the direction of her glance, went over to it and looked out.

"Looks clear, but I'll lock the door. Don't worry, I won't hurt you — I'll get my wife." He called out, "Gwynn, can you come downstairs, please," while walking into another small room, returning with a glass of water. As Sarah gulped it down, she could hear footsteps on the stairs and a woman appeared. She had fair hair and a kind face, and was wearing a large apron that wrapped right around her small frame, tying at the front, with large pockets holding hefty-looking scissors, and threaded with heavy duty needles.

"Who do we have here?" she asked.

"I'm Sarah."

"Well, hello, Sarah, I'm Gwynn and this is my husband, Corrin. What's happened to you? You look like you've been having a rough time. Have you hurt yourself?"

"It's my shoulder. I hurt it yesterday and when I jumped from the truck, I had to roll on it — it's really sore."

"Let's have a look." She eased back Sarah's shirt, took one look at the vivid purple bruise and asked her husband to go and get some ice. "Actually, how about coming upstairs — you're looking pale and clammy and you probably need to lie down."

As they helped her up the stairs, Corrin told his wife what had happened. By the time she was stretched out on the couch, she was shaking all over with shock, and Gwynn propped pillows behind her, pulling up a rug to cover her legs, even though the day was warm. Corrin brought ice, wrapped in a cloth, for her to hold on her shoulder, while Gwynn made her a cup of tea.

"When did you last eat something?"

"Umm... yesterday morning, I think, other than some berries last night."

Gwynn nodded to Corrin, who went to the kitchen, returning with a crunchy bread roll with a thick wedge of cheese and tomato in it. It was the best food she'd ever tasted! When her shaking subsided, she sat up and looked around at the homely room — it looked lived in and comfortable. Gwynn and Corrin were watching her, and when she started to speak, Corrin said "No, not now. It can wait. Why don't you have a wash — you'll feel better, then you can have a rest for an hour or so."

Gwynn took her to a small bathroom, where she washed her face and arms and hands. The water swirling down the plughole was a dirty greyish brown. Looking at herself in the mirror she saw a different person — tanned, with a few freckles appearing across her nose, but with spooked-looking eyes and fear written somehow onto her face. She remembered reading 'Inkheart' last year, and the bit about how people who were read into their world had words written on them — she imagined that was how she looked — that everyone could read her terror.

Her hair looked matted and mangy, so she shook it loose out of her ponytail and ran damp fingers through it. Gwynn handed her a comb, but then took it back, instead gently drawing it through her hair, untangling it for her.

"You remind me of my daughter. She's older than you and is away at university — she has wavy fair hair and blue eyes like you. Well, like me too, I guess." She took her back to the couch, where she helped her to lie down, tucking the blanket back around her. The last thing Sarah remembered was smiling at her, before dropping into a deep, exhausted sleep.

*

Sarah woke to the sound of hushed voices murmuring from the other side of the room.

"... sort of trouble? She looks like she's been sleeping rough and obviously felt she had to take a risk getting a ride with such an unsavoury character. I think I recognised the truck. It may belong to a man who works north of here — I've seen him selling fruit at the market. I wonder where her parents are."

"Well, gently does it — we don't want to sound like an inquisition and scare her. I've been thinking about our Aileish — if she was in trouble, we'd hope there was someone out there to look out for her. If you want to make sure she's all right this afternoon, I think I can finish off the order. I just have a few holes left to punch into the shoulder straps and into the extra belts they ordered... Look, I think she's stirring."

Sarah opened her eyes to see their concerned expressions and did her best to summon a wan smile. Everything had caught up with her and in the wake of their warmth and care, she felt as if she wanted to collapse into it and never get up again.

"Hello, Sarah, how are you feeling?" enquired Gwynn.

"Like I've been run over by a train! I know I have to pick myself up and keep going, but I'm exhausted and feel sort of flat."

"Keep going where?"

"It's a long story and I'm not sure whether I should tell you all of it because you'd only worry about things that only I can deal with."

"That sounds like a heavy load for a young girl to carry!"

Tears came to Sarah's eyes. She felt so close to giving up, as if all her courage and willpower had evaporated. Somehow, it was easier to keep going when people weren't so kind. She steeled herself. "I'm okay, I just have to go and get my bike from the village square and go back to find my friend, Tom. I'm hoping he's all right — that's probably why I'm so worried."

Gwynn and Corrin exchanged a look. Corrin said, "Well, I'm going with you to get your bike and to make sure you set off safely to find your friend. You know where we live if you need a place to stay, or if you just need to see friendly faces. And, one day, you might want to tell us your story — I'm sure it's an interesting one! I'm guessing your parents aren't in these parts for some reason to help you out, so please know you can call on us any time!"

Sarah just shook her head, not trusting herself to say anything without her voice breaking.

When Gwynn said goodbye to her, she slipped a leather bag over her shoulder, saying she'd put 'a little to keep her going' in it. It felt quite heavy. Gwynn wrapped her in a warm embrace that felt so good she didn't want to leave, but she reluctantly said goodbye and went out through the shop with Corrin. When he'd checked that the way was clear, he led the way back down Landing Road and turned into Market Street. They walked side by side along the road, talking about the town, Corrin's work and his daughter. When they drew near to Rose Road, Sarah must have become noticeably more vigilant, because Corrin gave her sidelong glances to make sure she was okay as they continued up Market Street. Every now and then he dropped a few questions into their conversation, which she mostly side-stepped, though she did find herself talking about meeting the Birches and how nice they were.

"Yes, we know of them, but they're not personal friends. Gwynn and I are always so busy keeping up with orders that we don't get out much. They run the mill called Riverstone, don't they?"

"Yes. I'm going to go there when I've found Tom."

"What do you mean 'found' him? Is he lost?"

"No... well I know where he is... It's just complicated."

They walked in silence for a while until Corrin quietly said, "Please don't forget, we're both here for you if you need us. I can sense that much more is going on than you can talk about just now."

It was strange seeing the village square without all the market stalls. It still had a few people wandering across it, but without the bustle she felt very exposed. The riot of colour, noises, smells and clusters of animated conversations of yesterday (*was it only yesterday...?*) had been enticing, and at the same time gave her cover as she sought to avoid Willard and Morwyn. Now, she felt vulnerable as she crossed the square to the bushes at the far side where she'd hidden her bike, the map and what was left of her provisions. Ryder wasn't anywhere to be seen, but she knew he would find her. They reached the trees and Sarah retrieved her bike and belongings before walking back across the square together, with Sarah wheeling the bike. They'd reached the beginning of Market Street when she saw Ryder flying in an arc across the sky. He swooped down towards her.

"My, he's a handsome creature. You don't often see hawks this close to the town," Corrin said, almost to himself.

As Ryder drew near, he said just one word, "Willard." Sarah looked around and blanched. There he was, walking past the town hall.

"The hawk's my friend and he's warning me. I'm sorry, Corrin, I have to go."

She swung herself onto the bike, wincing as she pulled on the handle bar with her sore arm, and pushed off down Market Street. Corrin looked in the direction of her gaze and saw a tall man with dark hair and a slightly stooped posture looking towards her, first registering puzzlement, then comprehension. He broke into a run, clearly intending to follow her down the street. As he drew near, Corrin neatly stuck out his foot and the man went flying, falling heavily on the cobblestones.

"Sorry!" exclaimed Corrin, grinning as he turned away. The man groaned and took a long time before trying to get to his feet.

Sarah glanced back and, seeing Willard face down on the ground, gave Corrin a big smile and a half salute before pedalling off as fast as she could on the uneven paving. She knew that once she got past the bridge she could ride quickly. Willard didn't have a vehicle and he couldn't run as fast as she could ride, and he wouldn't really know for sure that she was the girl he was after — he must have recognised her by Dervla's description. She smiled again to herself, thinking about Corrin tripping Willard up, feeling emotional about the very good people she'd met over the last few days. It was funny how, at home, she didn't really notice the good in the world. Maybe she was so caught up in her 'home bubble' — what was going on in her family and at school — that she hadn't really seen what else was out there. Or, maybe it was something to do with what Hermione had said, that if she had the right attitude, help would be there when she most needed it.

*

Once she was on the open road, riding was much easier, but after a few miles, as the adrenalin from needing to get away wore off, Sarah realised just how much her shoulder was aching. In fact, her whole body felt like it had had enough, and she began to think that relentlessly pushing herself on, now that she was out of immediate danger, might not be the best thing to do. She found a small cluster of trees where she could hide herself and the bike, and plonked down on the grass. Stretching out on her back to give her body a rest, she noticed that the sky had clouded over, indicating that the settled weather she'd come to expect was indeed beginning to change. Her stomach rumbled and she rifled through the panniers to see what she might have left to eat. Not much! She had half a container of water and an apple. *Oh well, better than nothing!* She then thought to look in the leather bag she'd been carrying over her shoulder since Gwynn gave it to her and hadn't had a chance to look inside. What treasures! A sandwich, a chunk of fruit cake, some plums and a small jar with a hand-written label saying 'skin balm' — and a comb. Now the weather was changing she might not burn any more, but her skin felt dry and rough, so the balm felt wonderful when she stroked it onto her arms and neck, her skin greedily sucking up the moisture.

Sarah had a snack and some of the water and set about repacking the panniers, deciding to put all the remaining food and her cardigan in them to make her shoulder bag easier to carry with just the water and the comb. Then, remembering the container of honey, she unrolled her waistband and took her first proper look at it. It was the same container, obviously, that she'd held before, but was somehow now imbued with so much more significance that it seemed different. She carefully opened it and gazed down at the golden fluid it contained. It wasn't clear — it was a thick, syrupy looking substance, with small crystals gathering on the sides of the container. It looked so benign, just like ordinary honey, though she was used to either the runny honey she used on pancakes, or the stiff clover honey her mother kept in the pantry.

Before she realised what she was doing, she put her little finger in it and lifted it to her mouth, licking it with the tip of her tongue without thinking. With a shock, she reminded herself that this was no ordinary honey. It was a special elixir that had caused at least two people she knew to do horrible things to obtain it. She quickly wiped her finger on the grass, but the honey's pull was almost magnetising. She imagined she felt a flood of good feeling washing over her, and it beckoned her to have some more. What would it matter if she had just a little bit? Should she keep some 'just in case' for the future? Maybe if she ever got home her mother would feel better if she had some? Could she take some for her? With enormous difficulty she pulled up her thoughts. What was the matter with her? She didn't want the honey, or what it might make her become, but it was pulling at her so seductively. Maybe it was a bit like Gollum and the ring in 'The Hobbit'? She quickly snapped the lid of the container shut and buried it in the bottom of her shoulder bag, getting to her feet and picking up the bike to stop herself from thinking about it.

Soon after she resumed cycling, she spotted Ryder high above, heading in her direction. She got off the bike and waved at him so he'd know she wanted him to land. He slowly drifted down to alight on a fence running alongside the road.

"Hi, Ryder. Are you okay? I was wondering when you'd show up."

"I was making sure Willard didn't follow. He fell hard, thanks to your friend, and was disoriented when he got up. He looked around as if he might try to get a ride with someone, but in the end stomped off back to his house."

"Thank goodness for that! He was really scary — thanks for the warning... Ryder, I wonder whether you could fly ahead to the treehouse and find Hermione, the grey cat. She's my friend and if she knows I'm on my way back, she'll let Tom know and will warn us about what Morwyn might be doing. I presume you can talk to her?"

"A cat? I haven't tried — they're usually too big for me to pay any attention to, though the odd cat baby has come my way."

"Ohhh, Ryder, that's awful! I think you're winding me up. Hermione is special, and definitely too big to be your prey. Please find her — she'll be somewhere in the trees near the treehouse."

Ryder flew off in the direction Sarah was headed, in the circling pattern of flight she'd come to expect from him. She imagined he had excellent sight and was checking out anything that moved over a wide radius. She didn't think small prey would stand much of a chance! She wished she could fly herself over the remaining miles. The break had refreshed her a little (*or was it the honey...?* she thought momentarily), but she was weary of the whole adventure and would love to be curled up somewhere safe and clean and comfortable with one of her new friends. It was funny that it wasn't her parents she wanted. She seemed to have left them behind for now. Maybe they'd been too distracted to really see and care for her for a while. It was as if they treated her as a child they couldn't share 'adult' things with, but at the same time abandoned her by keeping her at a distance. She understood more now about what it might be like for them being anxious or stressed, but she still wanted them to be there for her. When she got back (if she got back?) she wanted to talk to them in a way she hadn't been able to before. Maybe they just needed to talk more and be there for each other. She didn't feel as mixed up about it all any more, now that she'd had to handle much bigger things for herself.

She set off again on the final leg of her return journey to the treehouse.

Chapter IX
A Gathering Storm

It didn't seem to take long to cover the remaining distance to the turnoff to Morwyn's house. Sarah's thoughts had pushed her along and distracted her so she hadn't really noticed the ache in her shoulder. Maybe that tiny taste of nectar had helped. Wouldn't it be wonderful to have a pick-me-up available whenever she needed it? She shook herself — that was a dangerous thought. She made herself visualise the agony of Gollum, torn between desire for the ring and at the same time hating it, and what the power of the ring had done to him; how grovelling and sneaky he'd become.

As she turned the bike off the main road, the wheels juddered in the ruts of the smaller road, making her teeth chatter in her head. The front wheel regularly skidded sideways as it hit the loose gravel and she had to focus really hard to keep upright. When she got to the corner where she'd fallen off leaving the treehouse a few days ago, she decided to get off the bike and wheel it around the corner. As she walked, she realised how bone-tired she was, and that the dull ache in her shoulder really was annoying. It seemed incredible how much had been packed into those days, and the tension wasn't about to be over. She didn't want to think too much about what would happen next, because she didn't want to lose her nerve.

Hearing a call, she looked up to see Ryder flying over her, drifting in wide arcs, lower and lower. It looked like he was coming down to land just over the trees ahead of her. She kept wheeling the bike around the next, gentler, curve, and saw Ryder and Hermione on the grass verge waiting for her. She dropped the bike and ran over to pick up Hermione.

"Oh, Hermione, it's so good to see you!" Hermione rubbed her head around Sarah's neck, leaning into her, purring. When at last she put her down, they moved away from the road into the surrounding bushes, hiding the bike with them in case anyone happened to use the road. They spent a lot of time catching up on the events of the past few days, with Hermione reassuring her that Tom was okay and learning to talk to her. There was no hurry because Morwyn wouldn't be expecting her back until the following day at the earliest, and they were better to plan their next moves and get a rest before confronting her. While she'd known about their arrival in the land, her powers had been steadily decreasing, which was why she was so desperate for the elixir, and she was unlikely to know that Sarah was near.

Sarah made herself comfortable on the ground with the bike pannier as a cushion and ate most of the rest of her supply of food, leaving just a little for the morning. Ryder seemed to have been raiding Morwyn's garden and had left her a small pile of fresh, delicious tomatoes that he must have brought there one at a time. There was plenty of water in the stream, where she had a good wash and quenched her thirst.

They decided that it would be good for Hermione to go with

Sarah to keep Morwyn on the back foot, as she was known to hate cats, but to keep Ryder's existence quiet as a back-up if they needed it.

"I think we should hide the casket somewhere, because if I take it with me and give it to Morwyn, there's no guarantee she'll let Tom and me go," Sarah suggested. "She might keep us locked up — or worse, she might kill us, since we'll have outlived our usefulness. Keeping it away from her is the best way we can make sure we can swap it for Tom. If there's any way, I can avoid giving it to her altogether, I will, but not at the expense of our safety."

Hermione agreed that they'd find somewhere to hide the elixir in the meantime.

"I've been wondering…" Sarah said, "What harm could it do if she was to have the elixir?"

"Some say that the dark magical arts are rising and trying to return to our land. If Morwyn was returned to her natural powers and youth and vitality, she would be an ideal conduit from this side of the barrier."

"What barrier, Hermione?"

"It's a long story, and one best told after you've got through tomorrow. But you're right; if we can keep it from her, it may be better in the long run."

"And I don't want her to get her way after all she's put us through!"

"It's time for you to get some sleep so you'll be fresh tomorrow. I'll stay with you for a while, but Ryder and I have other things to attend to tonight. Don't worry, you'll be safe."

Sarah curled up on her foliage bed with Hermione between her arms and slipped into a physically and emotionally exhausted sleep... *She was walking in the countryside, through a meadow a bit like the one by the river where she'd found Tom. It was a beautiful day, sunny and warm, a light breeze rippling the long grass she was walking through. Ahead she saw some trees with a wooden seat in their shade and she decided to sit down to rest. As she sat there with her eyes closed a woman's voice roused her, asking if she could sit down beside her. When she opened her eyes, she saw a radiantly beautiful woman, wearing a light, silky dress, with long reddish-golden hair and piercingly green eyes. She was so beautiful she was mesmerising. Sarah just stared at her as the woman said that she'd been told she was a very special girl and was to escort her to a wonderful world where she would want for nothing and would stay young forever. Sarah started to say, "But what about...?" but found she couldn't speak. In a daze she found herself powerless to resist and walked beside the woman into the trees, further and further, until they were so close together their branches were overlapping and the sunlight was cut out. It became dark and hushed. She could only hear their footfalls and her own breathing, which became ragged as she grew more and more anxious. Suddenly, the woman disappeared and Sarah took another step in the dark — into nothing! She fell into an abyss. She was falling, falling, feeling cold air rushing past her and then she was on the ground in a dark cavern. As her eyes got used to the dark, with the help of a tiny shaft of light from above she could vaguely see that she was far underground, standing on a worn, rocky plateau, and she could hear a stream flowing somewhere below. She could just make out her hand in front of her, and stretched it out to touch the cold stone of the side of the cavern. Her skin prickled. She could feel something... something malevolent that was approaching. She screamed, the jagged noise reverberating off the sides of the cavern.*

She woke herself up in terror, to find herself lying on the ground, curled up in a ball grasping her legs, her breath coming in shallow gasps. She tried to breathe deeply and when she'd gathered herself together a little, sat up, grateful it was only a dream. But the feeling of terror remained. She wondered whether she'd screamed out loud and looked around — she was on her own — Ryder and Hermione weren't there. What was it about? The only thing she could think of was that perhaps the seductiveness of the woman was a warning to stay away from the pull of the elixir.

Suddenly, Hermione ran through the foliage to where she was sitting.
"I thought I heard you call in distress, but here you are, unhurt. What happened?"
"Oh, Hermione, I had a terrible dream and woke myself up with a fright. Where have you been?"
"Hunting, and checking on Tom. Morwyn has been treating him badly and I was worried about him yesterday, but he's sleeping now. So, tell me about your dream." Sarah recounted it to her, while Hermione solemnly listened. Sarah wondered how a cat could look 'grim' but by the time she finished, she could have sworn she had that expression on her face.
"What do you think, Hermione?"
"Well, you're probably right about the elixir. I think we would be wise to get Ryder to take it somewhere up high, out of the reach of humans, until it's the right time to do something

with it. But I wonder what else it might mean too; whether it portends something for the future."

Sarah only managed broken snatches of sleep for the remainder of the night. She woke in the dawn feeling disoriented and out of sorts. The weather seemed to be more overcast, with blustery clouds, and the wind was beginning to whip up and twirl around the leaves on the ground beside her. She finished the remnants of her food and had a quick wash in the river, noticing that it was a lot cooler than yesterday. She found herself feeling cross when Ryder took the container to hide it somewhere up a tree and Hermione went off to check on Tom. She knew she was being unfair and was taking out her anxiety on them, but she felt abandoned and alone. She spent a good bit of the time she was on her own feeling sorry for herself, until she stopped to think that maybe her ill humour was a result of her terror in the night. She couldn't let that risk her sabotaging the next few hours. It was too important to keep her wits about her if they were going to come out of it okay. So, she went for a walk, focusing on breathing deeply, on the movement of the trees, the sound of the river and the feel of the growing breeze on her skin. As she walked, she picked wild flowers and twisted them together into a garland that she put around her head.

Feeling restored, she returned to their hiding place to find they'd both returned. Hermione reported that Tom was well and was expecting their arrival in the early afternoon. Ryder had found a safe place for the container in a hole in the bark of a tall tree. He also warned them of an approaching storm — he could sense it in the air, and from above, he could see that black clouds were beginning to gather on the horizon.

They waited until a little after midday to begin their approach to the tree house, and, by then, the air was beginning to feel heavy and, Sarah thought, somehow cataclysmic.

"Time to go," said Hermione.

Sarah stood up, her legs suddenly wobbly. As she took a step, her pulse was racing and she wiped her sweaty hands on her tights.

"Stop a minute. Are you all right?"

Sarah couldn't answer. Her throat was dry and raspy and it felt like she'd swallowed a golf ball.

"Sarah, don't go into it feeling cowed. Stand as tall as you can and breathe deeply," Hermione instructed. "Can you get into contact with feeling angry about what Morwyn has done?"

Sarah nodded her head.

"Then hold that anger and use it to find your courage. Be that brave girl who's travelled so far in the last few days."

Sarah breathed deeply and stepped forward into the next part of her journey.

*

As Sarah and Hermione approached the clearing, with Ryder circling overhead, Sarah could see Tom working in the garden, bent over, pushing his dark hair out of his eyes. It looked as if he'd been pulling off planks of wood from the edging for the garden and had a stack of new ones on the ground ready to replace them with. He suddenly saw her and straightened up, nodding his head towards the shed to indicate Morwyn's whereabouts. He gave her a half wave of acknowledgement before taking a breath and calling out, "Sarah! You're back. I can't believe it — I thought you'd gone back to our world... Morwyn, Sarah's back!" He ran over to her, giving her a huge hug, being careful to ignore Hermione, as Morwyn emerged from the kiln. He whispered, "So glad you're back," before straightening up.

With barely supressed excitement Morwyn walked towards them. "Sarah, how lovely to see you again. I hope everything went well for you while you've been away. Oh... what's this you've got with you?" She stopped still and was looking at Hermione with a strange expression on her face. A mixture of fear and loathing. As Sarah and Hermione moved towards her, her eyes were fixated on Hermione, who arched her back and gave a ferocious hiss. Morwyn took a step backwards before gathering herself again and standing taller.

"It's so nice to see you," she said, obviously at a loss for words and repeating herself. "Why don't we go up to the house. You can leave the... cat here."

"No, Hermione is coming with me. So is Tom."

With an evil glare at Hermione, Morwyn lowered the ladder for them, maybe thinking that that would resolve the problem of the cat following, but Hermione quickly ran to the tree beneath Tom's window and disappeared. When they got to the deck, there she was, standing, looking smug and waiting for them. Sarah and Tom grinned at her and they all followed Morwyn inside.

Morwyn turned to face them, a strained look on her face. "Did you get it?"

Sarah just looked at her, wanting to make her squirm. There was a long pause.

"Well? Why aren't you answering me?" she demanded.

"Because I want you to tell me first how come Tom has made such a miraculous recovery when you told me he was dying?"

"What do you mean? My healing medicines worked better than I thought — isn't that marvellous?"

"Morwyn, we know that you were drugging him with Belladonna so that I'd think he was dying, to make me bring back the elixir for you. What do you want it for?"

"Did you get it?" Morwyn asked again.

"Why should I tell you? What will you do if I don't?"

"Don't push me, girl! You've got a bit uppity since you left, haven't you?"

As they were talking, Hermione was making a show of rubbing around Sarah's legs, and they were taking pleasure in Morwyn's obvious discomfort.

"So, what do you want it for?"

"That's my business, not yours!"

"But you had me risk so much to get it — I think you owe me an explanation."

"My, haven't you learnt how to be snippy! You should be grateful that I've helped you to grow up. So where is it?"

"Do you really think I'd be silly enough to bring it here with me? I need a guarantee of Tom's and my safety before you get your hands on it, otherwise we might just 'disappear'. I imagine you've probably tried this before — what's happened to the others? People seem to think there are a few kids from our world who've come to this one. Have you tried to use them too?"

"I don't know what you're talking about."

"I found some bones in the bank up the stream," blurted Tom. Morwyn went a bit pale and swung around to face him.

"I knew you'd be trouble. I should have kept you asleep. I could have given you more sleeping draught and told Sarah she was too late, so think yourself lucky!"

"What do you mean 'lucky', you mad witch? You drugged me, made me sick, locked me up and left me without food. Just how is that lucky?"

Through the skylights above them there was a flash of light, followed shortly after by a clap of thunder.

"That was close — about five seconds apart," commented Tom. They looked upwards, registering just how dark the sky had become. It was almost an inky, indigo colour, looking like a bruise in the sky, suddenly streaked again by another bolt of lightning. This time the bang was almost immediate and felt like it was directly overhead. Sarah jumped, then shivered, feeling like something was walking over her grave — she hoped that wouldn't literally be happening in the near future, but she felt a dark sense of foreboding. The wind was strong now too — the trees were swaying, carrying the treehouse with them in their dance, although it wasn't too scary since the trees were so large and solid. The timbers of the house creaked and groaned, and the slimmer branches whipped around, tearing at the windows, like dogs yapping and biting in their desire to get in.

While they'd been distracted, Morwyn had circled around behind Sarah and had just reached out to grab her, when Hermione's yowl pierced the room. Sarah dodged out of the way and instead Morwyn grabbed hold of Tom's arm. He hit out, trying to get away, but she slapped him hard across the face with her other hand. He froze and cowered, his body memory of past abuse completely knocking out his willpower. In that moment, Hermione launched herself at Morwyn's chest, all four paws stretched towards her, claws out, with a hideous cry, ripping, tearing and biting. Morwyn was thrown backwards, but somehow managed to grasp the skin at the back of Hermione's neck, stumbled, stopped herself from falling, then ran with a struggling Hermione to the door and hurled her as far as she could off the deck.

For a moment everything went still. Sarah and Tom looked at each other in total shock and disbelief.

"No!!" Tom yelled as his fury overtook him, propelling him at a run towards her. He didn't know what he was going to do, it was totally instinctive, but he hurled himself at her, yelling out his grief and rage. He charged into her with all his might and as her foot caught on a box on the deck, almost in slow motion, she toppled off the deck backwards. A few seconds later they heard a dull thump as she hit the ground.

It was as if time stopped. Even the storm seemed to halt as they stood and looked at each other in horror! Just as suddenly, rain started to fall, slowly at first, but quickly becoming a downpour, and Tom fell to his knees and huddled on the floor. Sarah made herself go to the edge of the deck and look over. Morwyn was lying on her back, arms and legs spread-eagled, and her neck at a strange angle, caught against Tom's planks, piled at the edge of the garden. There was no sign of movement.

Sarah wrapped her arms around her middle and slumped down onto her knees on the floor near Tom, feeling a mixture of relief after all the events of the past few days, yet also guilt and horror, with a sense of responsibility for Morwyn's death. She stretched out a shaking hand to place on Tom's shoulder. He was on his hands and knees retching terribly. He felt complete shock from the violence of the past ten minutes. It overwhelmed him, making his body shake uncontrollably, but at the same time — and even worse — there was a creeping sense of enormous grief at what Morwyn had done to Hermione. She was his friend, and she was gone. He started sobbing and collapsed into a curled-up position on the floor, rocking and hugging his knees. He felt Sarah pushing the hair back from his brow and heard her talking to him in a soothing voice.

"Come on, Tom, you're okay, we're going to be okay. Morwyn's gone, so we don't need to be afraid any more. She was a mean witch of a woman, and you didn't push her deliberately. And don't forget that cats have nine lives and I'm betting Hermione hasn't lived all of those out yet."

That was the bit that got through to him and he perked up a little. Maybe she wasn't dead, maybe she had survived. He'd heard stories of cats surviving massive falls. He stopped rocking and slowly sat up, still feeling nauseous and clammy, but a small spark of his deeper sense of himself returned.

Sarah got up and went to the kitchen to make them both a cup of tea. Her mum said it was good for shock. She felt wobbly, and a bit spacey. They sat on the couch together sipping the hot drink and giving themselves space to calm down.

"Right, we need to go down to make sure she really is dead. I'll go if you need to sit here for a bit longer."

"No, we need to look for Hermione, so I'm coming too."

They went to the edge of the deck where they'd seen Morwyn activating the winch for the platform and also the catch to release the ladder, but they were both locked. Where would the key be? They couldn't get down any other way — it was too high. Sarah made to go inside and search through Morwyn's room, but Tom suddenly remembered where he'd seen it.

"I'm pretty sure she kept it in her pocket. So... it will be down there with her — what are we going to do?"

They sat for a few minutes, both trying to make their brains work again, until Sarah suddenly grinned. "You haven't met our other friend yet, have you? Come out here and meet Ryder."

They went back onto the deck and Sarah called out to the hawk. He screeched in return, in recognition of her call, and appeared from over the trees, gliding down in a loose spiral until he alighted gently beside them.

"Ryder, this is Tom; Tom, meet our new friend, Ryder — he's some type of hawk. It might take you a while to understand him; his voice is scratchier than Hermione's."

Tom just looked at him, feeling dazed. Everything was happening far too quickly. He didn't even begin to know how to respond to a hawk whom Sarah could obviously communicate with. All he could manage to blurt out was, "He looks like a Harrier hawk."

Sarah put her hand on his arm. "It's okay, Tom, just take a deep breath; everything's going to be all right... Ryder," she said, "We're a bit stuck up here. Would you be able to fly down to Morwyn please and see if she has a key in her pocket? As you can see, she's come to a bit of a sticky end!" He made a squawking sound that to Tom sounded remarkably like a laugh, and launched himself off the deck and floated gracefully down to the ground. Tom felt spacey too — everything was catching up on him, and it was all weird! He found he couldn't process his thoughts and couldn't think of anything to say other than that they had a lot to catch up on, not least of which was how Ryder came to be part of their adventure.

Ryder found the key and brought it to them. They descended using the platform, feeling too shaky to risk the ladder, given that it was still quite windy. They hesitantly went over to where Morwyn was lying. She was waxy pale and, when Sarah felt for her pulse, her skin was already cool. She reminded her of the figures at the waxworks at Madame Tussaud's in London. A trickle of blood had come out of one ear, now partly washed away by the rain. She was very definitely dead. Sarah gently lifted her head off the planks, straightening her body as best she could, pulling her skirt down to cover her legs, and brought her arms in beside her body. It seemed the least she could do. Tom was standing there, unmoving, just staring down at her, still in shock.

"Tom, it's okay. There's nothing more we can do for her. I think we need to look for Hermione now, then go up to the house, get dry, find some food and have a good talk. We have a bit of planning to do and we need to have clear heads."

Sarah straightened up, and together they turned and started scanning the ground in the direction Morwyn had flung Hermione. They were both feeling sick, hoping with every bit of hope they had, that they wouldn't find her body on the ground. They paced out the arc where they thought she could have landed — no Hermione, so they started breathing more easily, thinking that if she'd managed to get up from where she'd landed, then at worst she might just be injured. They took turns calling her as they walked, checking out the trees and undergrowth around the clearing. There was no sign of her. Sarah turned to Tom, "I think we need to stop now. We're soaking wet and need to change our clothes and have something to eat. I'll get Ryder to have a look for her." With heavy hearts they walked back to the platform and ascended to the treehouse. Sarah called out to Ryder and he flew off, circling the trees and surrounding area.

Over the next couple of hours, they sat in the living room, feeling more settled after a long catch-up and something to eat. Outside, the rain had eased and a watery glimpse of sun had started to squeeze through the clouds. They were both shaken by what had happened to Morwyn, but it was the knot of anxiety gnawing in their stomachs about Hermione that stopped them being able to relax, not knowing what had happened to her and whether she was okay. Tom had visions of her lying injured somewhere and never finding her, while Sarah had more faith in the ability of a cat to survive, but she knew she'd feel huge relief once she turned up again. They decided they couldn't stay at the treehouse, not with Morwyn lying below them. Neither did they want to shift her and bury her — it didn't feel like their job and if they did bury her, no one coming looking would know what had happened to her, if anyone cared... They decided to pack some supplies and the casket and head off to Riverstone on the bike, where Sarah knew Mary and Arthur would welcome them. But they couldn't possibly think of leaving until they knew whether Hermione was all right.

As they were talking about what they might need to take with them, they heard Ryder call from the deck, just as a bundle of grey fur shot through from the direction of the broken window in Tom's room and skidded to a halt before them. She wound herself around their legs, purring loudly. Tom scooped her up and hugged her, reluctantly passing her to Sarah, both of them patting her until Hermione decided she'd had enough and wriggled out of their arms to the floor. She made it known that she was extremely cross with the indignity of being tossed off the platform by Morwyn, and needed a bit of time to lick her metaphorical wounds. She strode haughtily over to the window and with a flick of her tail, disappeared over the sill.

*

Sarah decided that what she needed first was a good shower — by the time she came out of the bathroom encased in a towel, her image in the mirror looked several shades paler! Her hair felt light and wonderful, after being pretty much ignored for the past few days. She had a massive bruise on her shoulder — it was progressing nicely from the purple of yesterday, to purple with red and yellow tinges at the edges. She looked through Morwyn's clothes and found a clean shirt to put on, along with her least dirty pair of tights — Morwyn's skirts were all much too large and long for her. Even though she didn't really want anything to remind her of Morwyn, out of necessity she also pulled out a pale grey woollen jumper, as it was definitely cooler than the previous days had been.

"Hey, Tom, do you think they have seasons here? I wonder if it's heading for autumn?" She didn't get a reply, so she poked her head around the door to the living room to see him huddled again, this time on the couch. He was shivering. "Tom, are you okay? I think you might still be in shock — you're shaking!"

He didn't reply, so she went back to Morwyn's drawers and pulled out a coarse brown, woollen jumper and took it to him. She had to shake him to rouse him enough to put it on. Concerned, she made him another hot cup of tea and made him drink it while she sat beside him on the couch. She put her hand on his knee, and he flinched away. He was feeling really vulnerable, as if he was just holding onto his emotions by a thread. He was terrified of losing it and making a fool of himself. Maybe he'd crumple and never be able to pull himself together. Maybe Sarah would be embarrassed for him — he didn't want her pity! He tried to stay withdrawn, keeping very quiet and still as he had at home, but Sarah called to Hermione, who appeared at the window and made her way over to curl up on his knee. When he didn't respond, she kneaded his knee until he said, "Ouch, stop it, Hermione!" She then stretched up, standing on her back legs with her front paws on his shoulders and nipped him on the nose. "What was that for?"

"You need to rouse yourself. We still have work to do before you get to safety. I know you're feeling bad, but if it's about Morwyn, she had it coming; if it's about you, you have two, no three, of us looking out for you now and it's time you started to trust us!"

Tom suddenly had a strange feeling welling up inside him —

he wasn't sure what it was, but it felt delicious and he realised he wanted to laugh! He'd been taking himself so seriously, but really, he'd got away from Gerald and Morwyn, he had three wonderful new companions, and he'd learned so much from them already. The world (whatever this one was) was opening up to him in a way he'd never experienced before, so at least he could try to enjoy it. He stroked Hermione's soft fur and this time received a lick on his nose. He turned to Sarah and gave her a rueful half smile, to which she responded by smiling and pulling him to his feet, making Hermione jump to the floor, and giving him a hug. She suggested that he could busy himself finding food for their journey to Riverstone, while she looked about for what else might be useful for them to take.

As Sarah looked around the living room, her eyes alighted on the book she'd admired earlier with the rune on the spine. There was something about it that she'd felt really drawn to, so she picked it up and put it on the table, shortly followed by one of the botanical books — it was covered in a beautifully soft brown leather, with ridges on the spine picked out with gold leaf. She liked the idea of working with herbs — good herbs, not poisonous ones! The idea of making potions that were good for skin, or for things like soothing stings or bruises, was appealing. In fact, why couldn't she take some of the potions with her so she could experiment with them later? She went into the kitchen, where Tom had already piled up some food, and started to take down jars of lotions that had labels, being careful to steer clear of ones she didn't know, or that didn't clearly indicate their purpose. *Arnica* was an obvious one, *aloe vera* for cuts or burns, a poultice with peppermint for itching and burning from allergies, also ones for bee stings;

sun burn; mosquito bites; and sleep. This one was interesting — the label said 'Calming the nerves'. She thought that might be useful — maybe for her mother! In the cupboards there were many different sized containers, so she took the smallest she could find and scooped the lotions into them, finding string and paper tags to tie around their necks for labels. She smeared some of the arnica on her shoulder, although thinking it was probably too late to do much for the bruising. She rattled on the handle of the locked cupboard, but in the end, she thought, *You know what, I don't need to know what's in there. I'm just going to leave this place behind.*

Sarah and Tom had been working in silence, but eventually he turned to her. "Sarah, I'm really sorry — I've been wallowing in feeling bad, when I know you've had a huge amount to work through yourself. I've been feeling so scared that I might be like Morwyn, or like Gerald — I've been wondering if I have that inside me. It's a terrifying thought and it's pushed me right to the edge of something really dark and scary."

"That reminds me a bit of a dream I had last night," responded Sarah. "I was in the dark and I fell down a huge hole and kept falling, but eventually I landed safely at the bottom of a cavern. But the terrifying thing was the creature waiting for me, hidden in the dark!"

Tom nodded in agreement. "Maybe that could be frightening for me too, but I think that after all the things that have happened this week, maybe I've found the courage to face up to that 'creature' that was in Morwyn. I just freaked out that my actions had killed her. What I'm really afraid of, that's way worse for me, is the abyss, a big black hole where I'm alone and falling with no one to catch me or care for me, and it going on forever! But when I let myself think about it properly before, I realised I have a choice. I now have you and Hermione and Ryder, even though I don't always understand him yet, and I'm not alone. I know that we're in it together, and I need to stand tall and get on with it."

"And you'll have the Birches and Gwynn and Corrin — you'll meet them and trust them too," said Sarah, smiling for the first time since Morwyn's death.

They carried on with what they were doing for a minute in a companionable silence, then Sarah threw a couple of nuts at Tom. "Anyway, where did you find this stash? I love nuts and dried apricots. Nothing better for the next stretch of our journey. So much better than the scroggin stuff we had for school tramps!"

The containers and food were packed into the panniers, with their clothes stuffed in around them. Sarah put the books in her shoulder-bag, then changed her mind and swapped them for her clothes. Her shoulder was still tender and she didn't want to risk slowing them down on their way to Riverstone by loading it up too much. As they were about to leave, looking around for the last time, Tom suddenly went over to the pottery table by the window. He picked up one of the smaller figurines and stuffed it in his pocket. He thought it might be good for him to have a gargoyle to look at to remind him of what he'd encountered and overcome, in case he ever doubted himself in the future.

As Tom wheeled the bike between them away from the treehouse, they cast a last look backwards. It looked benign there, perched up high in the trees, yet so much had happened in the last week — it felt momentous. They didn't feel like the same kids they'd been when they arrived. They rounded the first corner and it was gone. Sarah reached her hand over and placed it on the handlebar beside Tom's, helping him to steer the bike on the gravel. They'd decided it would be too difficult to ride with one of them pillion until they got to the main road, so they walked quietly together on the rough road down to their turning. Hermione had told them she would make her way to Riverstone overnight and would see them in the morning; Ryder had flown on ahead to scout for any trouble. He'd also decided that once they were safe, he would take the container with the elixir from its hiding place in the tree up into the mountains in the north, with the idea of finding a safe place where it could be left, in case they needed it sometime in the future. The weather was still windy, with occasional squalls of drizzle, but the storm had passed, and with it all the tension they'd been living with for the past week.

Once they arrived at the main road, Tom said he'd ride the bike because of Sarah's shoulder, while she sat across the panniers on the back. The journey was uneventful; the road was quiet, and as they moved further into the countryside there was very little traffic. They stopped once for a snack, and drew near to Riverstone just as the sun was starting to dip down towards the horizon and shadows were lengthening beyond the trees.

"Look, Tom, there's Riverstone." Tom was quietly relieved. He hadn't said anything, but even though the distance hadn't been great, he was really tired. The road surface was good for a gravel one, but even though it was well compacted, he'd had to focus hard to make sure he avoided the odd stone that was sticking up, or ruts from over-zealous vehicles.

Normally, he loved bikes and could handle them easily, but with a passenger on the back it didn't respond as easily. As they drew nearer, the lights from the mill house showed through the curtains and looked welcoming — no more the abandoned house Sarah had stumbled into a week ago. When they drew up to the gate, they both dismounted and Tom wheeled the bike up the path to the base of a set of steps, leaving it propped against the stone wall of the house. The steps led up to a small landing that connected around a corner to the one Sarah had used to enter the house when she'd first arrived. Finding herself in front of the door again felt strange, and she hesitated before putting out her hand and rapping on the wood with her knuckles. They heard footsteps approaching the door, it was pulled open, and the smiling face of Mary was in front of them.

Chapter X
Belonging

Mary drew Sarah to her, giving her a warm hug, her face crinkled in a wide smile. As she let her go and stood back, Sarah introduced Tom.

"Mrs. Birch, this is my friend, Tom."

"Please call me Mary, Mrs. Birch sounds so formal. It's so good to see you again, and lovely to meet you, Tom. Please come in." She led the way into the living room, which was transformed from the abandoned and dusty shell Sarah had seen just a week ago. They found themselves in a warm and inviting room, with fresh flowers on the table and a fire burning in the fireplace, which, even though it wasn't very cold outside, made the room feel homely and welcoming. A book was lying open, upside down, on the table beside a mug, and wonderful smells were wafting down the hallway from the kitchen. Tom could feel his mouth starting to water.

"Sarah, you look like you've been through a lot since we saw you last! Maybe it's your tan... no, it's more than that — there's something in your eyes... Don't worry about talking just now. There's plenty of time for that. How about we go and surprise Arthur? He's in the mill room. You might find it interesting to see how the mill works while I finish off the dinner. I bet you're hungry." They followed her down the corridor leading out from the living room, to the large double doors opposite the kitchen that, last time she was here, Sarah had correctly thought must be the mill room. She pushed one of the doors open and they walked through to a large room. The first thing they both saw was the huge stone wheel at the end of the room. Tom was fascinated. The wheel was actually two round stones, one on top of the other. The top stone was slowly turning, connected by a big wooden gear wheel to a horizontal axle that went through the wall. *Of course*, he thought, *that's linked to the mill wheel outside and the river makes it turn.* While they watched, Arthur pulled on a giant lever and the top stone rose up. He then shovelled more grain onto the bottom stone and lowered the top one again. So simple, but so powerful. Tom was totally absorbed with the slowly turning axle, the angle of the gear wheel and the power of the turning stone. It was noisy, making a deep, rumbling sound. It wasn't until Arthur operated another gear to separate the horizontal from the vertical axle that it stopped, and in the sudden quiet he turned towards the door and saw them standing watching him. He wiped his hands on his apron and came over to meet them.

As Sarah walked towards him, he held out his hands and took hers between them. They were warm and strong and Sarah was reminded of her grandfather.

"Sarah! It's so good to see you safe and well. And you must be Tom." He turned to Tom and shook his hand. Tom was bursting with questions for him about the mill, but Arthur laughed, saying, "Hold on, plenty of time for questions. First things first — I'm sure you're hungry, I know I am. Let's have some dinner and you can tell us about your adventures. I'll show you how it all works tomorrow, Tom."

They sat at the wooden table by the fire for their dinner, and were served large helpings of roast chicken, potatoes, beans and broccoli, smothered in gravy. It tasted wonderful — the first proper, hot meal they'd had in a week. They were completely silent as they ate and Mary and Arthur waited until they finished, before suggesting they move to the more comfortable chairs by the fire to talk. Sarah and Tom filled them in on all that had happened since Sarah left them at Hunterdale. When they got to the part about Morwyn's fall their faces creased with concern. Arthur leaned over and put his hand on Tom's shoulder.

"We hope neither of you feels any sense of responsibility for this. When someone uses other people for their own ends as Morwyn has, they have to accept that it might not go their way. More often than not, there'll be a payback. It's just tragic that you had to be caught up in it. I'll go and deal with her in the morning. It's not anything for you to worry about any more — it was an accident that she brought on herself."

"We'd be very happy for you to stay with us just as long as you need to, so you can stop worrying about that too." Mary felt a welling up of emotion and looked at Arthur with tears in her eyes. Arthur reached out and covered her hand with his.

"We weren't able to have children of our own, so it's really nice to have you here with us." He got up and went into the kitchen, returning with a plum tart garnished with big dollops of cream. They'd thought they were full, but made space for the delicious, fresh and fragrant tart, then relaxed back into their chairs, gazing blearily into the fire.

"I bet you're tired. How about I take you upstairs and show you your rooms? You can help me make up your beds while Mary prepares a hot bath." He led them upstairs to the spare rooms. One faced over the waterwheel, the other had windows overlooking the road. They were quite small, but comfortable, and by the time they'd helped each other make up the beds and put away their meagre belongings, they felt more settled than they had been since they'd left home. Tom wondered whether he already felt more secure than he ever had before, even though their time in this world had been so uncertain. At least the Birches didn't mean him any harm! Mary came upstairs with flowers from the garden for each room.

"Sarah, how about you have the first bath? There's plenty of water for Tom to have one after you. I've found some pyjamas for you to wear for tonight. They'll be much too big for you, but if you give me all your dirty clothes, I'll have them ready for you tomorrow. They'll dry nicely in front of the fire."

Taking Sarah into the bathroom, she helped her out of her clothes, grimacing at the bruise that stretched across her shoulder and down her arm, and made sure the bath was the right temperature before leaving the room. Sarah lay back in the water and sighed. An enormous weight felt as though it was lifting. She'd been worrying and coping for the entire week and now it felt like she had others to share the worry with, and grown-ups who could help. The Birches were so nice. She felt her body relaxing into the water and slid down until it reached her chin, taking time to luxuriate in the warmth before soaping herself all over, including her hair. As she was emerging from the bath, Mary appeared with a large, fluffy towel and wrapped her in it, handing her pyjamas that were obviously her own, before emptying out the bath and refilling it for Tom.

Tom's turn in the bath left his spirits rising — he felt almost gleeful feeling the warm water on his body and realising how far away he was from Gerald. He couldn't reach him and would never hurt him, or shame him, again! His thoughts clouded though as Morwyn's demise came back to mind, although he knew rationally it had just been an accident. What was still disturbing though was the thought of Leah and his grandparents, especially the thought of them worrying about him, but he veered away from that — it was too hard for now and he had to start to trust that things would work out.

By the time they'd finished their baths they felt completely shattered. Sarah was briefly concerned about Hermione and Ryder, but even being worried didn't stop her from yawning and fantasising about what it would be like to curl up in a comfortable bed, after having to sleep on the hard ground for the past few nights. Arthur suggested that they could continue their questions tomorrow after a good night's sleep, and they were both asleep within minutes of their heads touching their pillows.

*

Tap, tap, tap. They looked up from the table where they were enjoying breakfast, hearing a tapping on the door. Mary went over and opened it, and with a shriek of happiness, Sarah jumped up and joined her, closely followed by Tom, seeing Hermione standing on the step with a stick in her mouth that she'd been using to knock on the door.

"Hermione!"

She dropped the stick and sauntered into the house.

"Well, hello, Hermione, I'm very pleased to meet you — I've heard a lot about you." Mary bent down and ran her hand down Hermione's back, to which she responded by raising the base of her spine up into Mary's palm.

"She loves that, in case you couldn't tell," commented Tom.

"Yes," Sarah added, "She says that humans are at their best when they're stroking her!"

"Did it take you long to be able to 'hear' her speaking to you?" Mary wanted to know.

"Sarah could do it almost straight away. I'm not so good at it, but I can make out most things now. I still can't really understand Ryder though — he's much squawkier, so I have to sort of watch him and the context, and imagine what he's trying to say."

"So, can I learn to understand her?"

Hermione gazed impassively at them, but flicked her tail from side to side.

Sarah smiled, "She says 'No, you're too old to learn'."

"Oh, well, we'll have to try something different then. Hermione, if I ask you a question and the answer is 'Yes' you could lift your right paw, and if it's 'No' you could raise the left. Does that sound like a good idea?"

Hermione casually raised her right paw, lifting it up to her mouth to daintily lick before lowering it back to the floor.

"Wow, that's incredible. Hermione would you like something to eat?"

Hermione lifted her left paw. Mary looked puzzled until Sarah said, "She says there are more than enough mice and rats in the grain store for one cat. I have to say, she said it with more than a hint of criticism! And she also said she's rather partial, though, to a bowl of milk."

Mary smiled. "This is amazing. I wish I'd known a long time ago that cats could communicate like that."

Hermione lifted her nose in the air, flicked her tail and walked off haughtily towards the kitchen.

"Is she miffed about something?"

"Ha, ha, she says she's not a normal cat! I don't think she likes to be compared to 'commoners'," Sarah laughed.

Mary followed Hermione down the corridor and disappeared into the kitchen with her.

Tom and Sarah tucked into poached eggs on toast, washed down with creamy hot chocolate. Tom suddenly realised that he'd completely forgotten to think about counting before he ate. He couldn't remember ever wolfing down a meal before. Even the night before he'd been too exhausted and unsure of himself to let go like this.

"It's funny how good the simplest things taste when you're not feeling anxious."

"So, why would you feel anxious about eating, Tom?" asked Arthur.

Tom hesitated. It was so hard to open up. Did these people really want him to answer honestly? It all seemed so big — where would he start? Maybe they just wanted a polite answer and would be embarrassed if he dumped on them.

"It's hard, isn't it? To talk about personal, emotional things," said Arthur. As if he could read his mind he added, "I find that things I feel bad about are better talked about with friends so I can get a better perspective on them, or else they fester inside me and get bigger until I feel like I'm going to explode."

Tom swallowed and suddenly everything was blurted out in a rush. "I wasn't just anxious about eating, it was everything! My dad died when I was four, and my mum remarried a bully called Gerald when I was six. He hates me! He takes out all his anger on me, sometimes on mum. Sometimes I think that even my breathing annoys him. Maybe that's just it — he'd rather have my mum to himself. I have an older sister, Leah, but she somehow manages to just blend in by doing stuff to keep the peace."

"That sounds terrible. Does he hit you?"

"…Yes," he replied in a small voice, his heart starting to race.

"What about your mum? Doesn't she try to stop him?"

"It's complicated. It's like she's glued to him somehow — she tries to please him all the time and even after he hits her, she says it was her fault and she deserved it. Most of the time she's so wired up to every move he makes she doesn't even notice Leah and me. It's all about her and how afraid she is, and what she has to do to please him."

"Did you have anyone you could talk to about it?"

"My dad's parents are great, but they won't let them see us. My mum's parents died in a car accident when she was young and she doesn't have anyone else. I think she was different when I was little, though I can't really remember. It's like she decided she wasn't worth anything more than being with someone horrible when dad died."

"Maybe she felt abandoned and couldn't cope on her own?"

Tom found he had a lump in his throat and knew that if he

tried to say anything, his voice would crack. He was fidgeting in his chair and could tell his chin was about to wobble — he hated people seeing him when he was feeling so vulnerable and open. Arthur put his hand on his shoulder. Don't be nice to me, just don't be nice to me, he thought, terrified that he would lose it, burst into tears and not be able to stop.

"You know, there's no shame in feeling emotional when you're thinking about bad things that have happened to you. It's okay to let people who care about you see that you're hurting. You may not be used to it, but we're all good people and we won't judge you or hurt you."

A few tears leaked out of the corner of his eyes, but the ground didn't open up and swallow him, and he was surprised to realise that some sort of weight had lifted off him. Just saying out loud how horrible it had been felt good. Sarah was looking at him with such a warm look in her eyes, like she really got him, not the look of horror he had expected. And Arthur had an arm firmly around his shoulders and felt so solid somehow.

He looked up and saw that Hermione had reappeared in the doorway. She looked very satisfied, standing there licking her paw, and running it over her face and whiskers.

"You look like the cat that got the cream!" he said, smiling at her. She sauntered into the room followed by Mary, who suggested that they move to the more comfortable chairs, indicating that Tom and Sarah could share the couch. Hermione jumped up between them, stretching along their legs looking, in Tom's view, like an Egyptian Sphinx, head up, paws stretched in front of her and somehow very regal.

Mary and Arthur settled into chairs and Mary started off the tale of how they came to be living there and what they understood about the land, North Feasgar. She told them that they'd both arrived there together from England when they were fifteen and sixteen, which took both Sarah and Tom by surprise. They looked at each other in astonishment — this wasn't what they were expecting at all, even though Sarah then remembered the coin Arthur had given her — it had completely gone out of her mind, and she suddenly realised she hadn't seen it since she got into the canoe. It had probably got lost when she fell out.

"How did it happen for you? Was it anything like how we got here?"

"We were both trying to get away from our families for a bit — they didn't approve of us being together — they said we were too young. So we went for a walk in the countryside for the day and found a steep bank overgrown with foliage. The earth had an opening in it, not really a cave, more like a sort of a crack, where we thought we could hide out for a while. We were curious, so we explored inside — it went back a long way but we could see a chink of light, so we made our way towards it and when we walked through the opening, we found ourselves here. We didn't even think to try to go back, and when we did, we couldn't find the opening. We floundered around by ourselves for a while, living rough, until we were taken in by a family with two young children. They were really kind to us and helped us until we were old enough to leave to go to the city. We decided to study there. We've never forgotten their help and we'd like to repay that debt by doing the same for you, for as long as you need us."

Tom and Sarah felt overwhelmed that they would be so

kind to them, although Sarah wasn't sure that she was ready to accept that she wouldn't be going back home. She felt teary and confused.

Arthur was talking, so she tried to swallow her emotions and focus on him. He was saying that North Feasgar was quite backward technologically, so he and Mary went to university thinking that they could maybe contribute to its future somehow, given that they had experience and knowledge from their other life. They both studied engineering, Mary to become a designer, while he was more interested in the practical side, to try to introduce some development in technology, but even now it hadn't really caught up with what they remembered from England thirty years ago. The country was cut off from the south, and external knowledge and goods couldn't be accessed.

"We worked in the city until we decided to change our lifestyle, buying the mill so we could work in the countryside. We still do a little of our old work when we feel like it, but we love the pace of our new life here," said Mary.

"We didn't find out that there was a possible way home until we were a lot older," Arthur added, "But by then our families had moved on. I had four brothers and three sisters and they were all caught up in their adult lives without me. Mary didn't want to go back, she's an only child and her parents gave every indication of not caring about her when she was there, other than being strict with her. She didn't want to go back and I wouldn't have gone without her, anyway."

"What way?" Sarah asked, but Tom interrupted. He'd been bursting with excitement about what Arthur was saying and was impatient to edge into the conversation.

"Wow, that's amazing — so that's why the cars are so old looking. And there don't seem to be any phones."

"There are phones in the city and towns, but they haven't run wires out to more remote places like this."

"But we don't have wires — don't you have Wi-Fi?"

Mary and Arthur exchanged a look that said they didn't have any idea what they were talking about.

"Our phones don't have wires," explained Tom, "Neither does my computer. They're connected through the ethernet." He tried to explain what the ethernet was.

"That's fascinating. When we left, there were obviously phones, and we did have computers but they were mostly used in businesses. We certainly didn't have one ourselves. What are they like?"

"Probably much, much smaller than anything you've seen. Even since I was little, they've become smaller and able to do much more, much faster."

"My phone is really skinny and fits in my palm." Sarah showed them what sort of size it was. "It's called an iPhone and all of us have them."

"Well, not quite all of us," chipped in Tom. "My grandparents gave Leah and me one so we could keep in touch with them but Gerald was so wild he took mine, threw it on the floor and stomped on it. I've never been able to afford to get another one. Leah's just 'disappeared' one day…"

"I'm sorry to hear that you've had such a bad time with your stepfather — he sounds like a complete bully."

Tom swallowed and couldn't say anything past the tightening in his throat.

Arthur realised Tom needed them to just keep talking as

normal — it was obviously very hard for him to confront the hurt from his background, so he carried on talking about how he and Mary weren't able to help develop that kind of technology as they didn't have knowledge or skills in communications. He asked them to explain to him, what they could do with their phones and computers, and was completely taken aback that they could send messages on their phones as well as call. When Sarah told them that they could see each other when they made calls, he remembered that someone had suggested once, when he was young, that one day they'd be able to do that and how far-fetched he'd thought the idea was. Neither of them could really understand, though, when Tom tried to explain about modern computers, the internet, the massive amount of data they could access and the speed with which they could do it. Mary felt as if they were sitting there with their mouths wide open, unable to imagine the possibilities this offered.

"But my parents are always telling me about the bad things about phones too," Sarah explained. "They think we spend all our time looking at them instead of focusing on school work, and they worry that I might get run over because I look at the screen when I'm walking rather than watching where I'm going. Or, they think that when I'm listening to music, I might not hear a car and get hit. They're also afraid that I'll get cancer, or something, from having my phone against my ear too much, but that's just silly because I hardly ever actually talk to anyone on it, except them, because we all just use it for texting."

"But, the best thing about not having one is that no one can bully me with it," Tom said. "Some of my mates get a really hard time."

"So, how does that work?"

"It seems stupid sometimes to text someone on the other side of the room when we could talk, but that's what everyone does. It's supposed to be more private, but sometimes people you trust do dumb things and send what you've written to all sorts of people or, even worse, a picture of you doing something stupid. When it's out of context it can make us look really bad. They sometimes tag them with horrible messages about how we look, or what losers we are."

Arthur and Mary just looked at each other and didn't say anything. It sounded terrible, but it was obviously the environment they were used to and it wasn't their place to comment.

To fill the sudden gap in the conversation, Mary did her best to fill in their understanding of the history of Feasgar. "About one hundred years ago, we've been told that there was a major uprising in the land, that included more than double the area of what we currently call North Feasgar. At that point, magic was common and a group of sorcerers located south of Greyvyn, had mastered the dark arts and were training a large force of men to overtake the north using dark magic to support them. Everywhere they advanced brought bloodshed and destruction."

"Sounds like a fantasy movie," commented Tom, "Though, in the movies the goodies always win!"

Arthur picked up the tale, "The sorcerers in the north sacrificed the power they had to erect a magical barrier between the northern and southern lands. It created a complete severing from the rest of the world as it was known, keeping what is now North Feasgar safe, but secluded. It has meant that we haven't been able to develop in the same way we might have. We have one main city, which is some way east of Hunterdale, but no information, interaction or materials from outside. We've had to make do with what we can work out and create ourselves."

"Oh, so that's why you use steam cars instead of petrol!" Tom exclaimed.

"Well, you see, we don't even understand how to acquire petrol, let alone how to use it, even though the two of us remember its presence from our childhood... And steam is cheap and easy to harness and use here, as you'll have seen where it spontaneously spews out in the area around Hunterdale. So, we're two of a very small number of people who have studied engineering at the only university in the land and have the skills Willard needs to develop a flying machine, to get him to the honey. We're the only two in the Hunterdale area, and since we refused to design and make it, he kidnapped us."

"What about Morwyn? Didn't she have some magical powers?" Sarah wanted to know.

"The small amount of magic left in the land seems to have been passed on to a few, but it isn't much more than the Sight and thought-sharing," Mary said. "Morwyn also cultivated knowledge of natural lore for her lotions and potions, but used it selfishly. In a society where 'bad' has been removed, people will still gravitate to different types of behaviour true to their personalities — Morwyn was self-serving and wanted power, and drove herself to wrong-doing. She had to stay youthful at all costs to satisfy her view of herself."

"The problem is," Arthur continued, "When there's a

tightly closed system, as we have here, existing within a more open world, there has to be a build-up of tension. We think that's why small tears, or rifts, have occurred between here and our original world. So far, the few people who have come through have been young — whether that's because they're small, or have a quality of innocence, or imagination, we can only guess. We wonder, too, how long the barrier will hold up against the south, as their magic and use of technology will have grown at a much faster rate than ours."

They both listened, fascinated — Tom thinking about all the implications for living and working in North Feasgar; Sarah worrying about what might happen if the dark powers broke through to the land. Tom had a sudden thought, "So, the UK and New Zealand are almost directly opposite each other if you look at a globe, aren't they?"

"Yes..."

"And you two and Sarah come from England, and I'm from New Zealand. There don't seem to have been any other random people popping in from, say, Russia or China... What if the rift happens somewhere along a line connecting the two countries? They're a similar land size and New Zealand Europeans mostly come from the UK — wouldn't it be funny if they were somehow connected in another dimension as well?"

"Hmmm... Well, you're a clever lad, aren't you? Any other strangers reported have been English speaking, but I've never been told more than that. They haven't stayed here for long, although Morwyn may have had something to do with that...! That's a really interesting idea."

They had a whole lot of other questions to ask, but Arthur

reminded them that he had to head off to the treehouse to dispose of Morwyn's body, and wondered whether Tom might be willing to go with him to help. One part of Tom wasn't keen at all — he felt a mix of scared and guilty, but another part of him knew it was important to face it and let it go, so he agreed, trusting in Arthur's solid presence to make sure he was okay. He told Arthur that there were spades in the shed there, so they disappeared out the door to where Arthur had a small truck tucked around the back of the house, leaving Mary and Sarah to clear away the breakfast, supervised by a superior looking Hermione who watched on from a sunny patch in the living room.

When they were in the kitchen, Sarah asked Mary what she'd meant when she said there was a way to get home.

"When we first moved to this area, we saw the labyrinth on a map and, by asking around, we found out that folklore said that if you travelled to the centre of the labyrinth in the right frame of mind, or maybe with the right personal qualities, there was a pool that would show you what you needed to do in the immediate future. No one I met had ever gone there, maybe out of fear about what they would find, or possibly because they didn't understand the power of the labyrinth walk and confused it with a maze? Anyway, we both decided to go together, and it was clear when we looked into the pool that we needed to stay."

"How could it show you that?"

"It was a long time since we'd left and we could see our families getting on with their lives, with no evidence at all of our presence... We were also shown that two young people would appear in the future, though we didn't see clearly what you would look like, and that the four of us have a task to complete that is vital for the land."

Sarah felt worried and confused about what this meant for her. She was torn. If she and Tom could find their way to the labyrinth, should she stay or should she go? She wanted to see her family, but didn't want to leave Riverstone. Did this mean she had to stay? If she did, what about her parents, her grandparents? Her emotions started to spiral, and it must have shown on her face because Mary put her arm around her and did her best to calm her down.

"Sarah, it will be okay. Trust that whatever the pond reveals, that will be the right thing to happen, at the right time. Even if you have a task to complete here, that doesn't mean you won't have the chance to return home as well. The thing is not to worry — just know that whatever you do, it will turn out to be the right thing because the labyrinth knows what your qualities are and what you're here to do."

"But, what about Tom? And the rest of you?"

"How long have you been here now?"

"Well, yesterday I worked out we'd been here six days, so a week?"

"Maybe you need to think about the fact that, somehow, at home you've gone missing. I don't know how it plays out; maybe time is different here to what it is there, but I don't think so. When we had a glimpse of our families, they'd aged in much the same way we had. So, we can't be sure what will have happened for you at home — but by now your parents will be very worried. I'm thinking that if it's right for you to go back, it will need to be soon. Don't worry about Tom — I don't imagine that he'll want to return, and we'll take care of him, and I'm sure that we'll be seeing you again! I've been thinking too about the way you both got here. I'm guessing that each of us has a unique portal into this world. I can't imagine how Tom could recreate his entry — how he could replicate his slide down the hill into the river and the bump on his head. You, though, have a way here that you could reproduce, in much the same way Arthur and I could have if we'd known how to return."

Sarah was overcome with emotion — that she'd done so much already, that she still had something important to do in this land, and that she had met such wonderful people here who she already felt connected to. And, of course, there were Hermione and Ryder. Ryder…

"Oh, my goodness, I'd forgotten about Ryder. He said he'd be here by daybreak and it's midday. How could we have forgotten to look out for him?"

She went outside, feeling guilty and distressed. Looking into the sky she rotated in a circle, looking to the horizon in all directions. The sun was high, the air balmy, everything looked calm and benign, but there was no sign of Ryder. It felt wrong. Mary came out behind her and checked as well. There was no sign of him.

"Don't worry, Sarah, he's probably just hunting. Come inside and help me prepare some food for when Tom and Arthur return."

"But he promised he'd be here — he told me he likes hunting in the evening mostly."

Mary put an arm around her shoulders and gently steered her back to the house. "Worry won't bring him back. If he's not here when Arthur's back, we'll make a plan to go and look for him, although if he was flying to the mountains in the north, it might be like looking for a needle in a haystack."

Back indoors, Mary started to sort things out in the kitchen. She wanted to keep Sarah occupied so that she didn't dwell on Ryder too much.

"Tell me about your family, Sarah," she asked.

"Well, there's just mum and dad and me. Mum's a teacher, though she hasn't worked much over the last year or so. I think she just does relief work when she feels like it. Dad manages a computer graphics company. He must be really busy, because he's not around much. They don't really talk to me about what's going on, but they're not happy. I can feel it, and just before I left, dad said he had to have a break for a while. I don't even know what that means — whether he's leaving mum or what."

"I'm so sorry, Sarah. That must be awfully confusing."

"I think it's something about mum. She's been really sort of remote and unhappy for quite a while. And they don't talk about it so there's a kind of atmosphere in the house. It's thick and heavy, and I don't know what to do about it."

"Could she be depressed, do you think?"

"Maybe. Does that feel like all the energy is being sucked out of the room? I try to make things better by being helpful, making cups of tea, trying to think of things to say when dad's around, but it's exhausting and I can't fix it, and I feel sick all the time. Sick-nervous, not ill. It's like mum has something around her, a barrier that I can see through, but I can't touch her and she can't touch me."

"Like a membrane?"

"Yes, she's in a bubble, a grey bubble. I don't know where

dad is — he's not in there with her, but he's not with me either."

"It does sound to me like she's depressed — that creates huge pressure in a family, for your dad as well, especially if he doesn't know what to do to help her. It's much harder for sensitive kids to deal with, and I think you're intuitive, so you'll notice an atmosphere maybe even more than they do."

"How do you know so much about it?"

"My dad was depressed. He coped, by drinking too much, and when he drank, he got angry with us."

"What about Arthur? Did he have stuff going on in his family too?"

"Why do you ask?"

"I was just thinking — maybe all of us who come here have had something going on? Maybe just kids who're unhappy find their way through a rift? Maybe happy kids don't have any reason to, or their energy isn't right or something?"

"Well, that's an interesting thought!"

Mary and Sarah carried on getting the food ready in silence, both contemplating the conversation they'd just had. Neither of them had talked that way to anyone before, and each could feel a bond growing between them, but neither was ready yet to talk about that out loud.

*

An hour later, Sarah was pretending to set plates and cutlery on the table, while anxiously pacing backwards and forwards to look out the open door. She'd just turned back into the room for the umpteenth time when she heard a distant screech. She raced out the door and looked up. The day was bright, with just a few sparse wisps of white cloud stretched out over the blue sky. She couldn't see anything until she heard the sound again, and with her hands shielding her eyes from the sun, she could just make out a dark speck approaching from the north.

"Mary, it's Ryder!" she shouted. As he got closer, though, she could see there was something wrong. One of his legs was dangling down in a strange fashion and his flight wasn't as sure and smooth as usual. "Mary, please come — I think there's something wrong with him."

Mary ran outside in time to see Ryder swoop in lower and lower, and eventually sink down to land in an ungainly way on the grass. Racing over to him, Sarah threw herself down on the grass beside him.

"Ryder, what's wrong? What's happened to you?"

His speech was raspy and scratchier than usual, and quite hard to understand, but Sarah made out that he'd been nearing the base of the mountains when he saw smoke rising from a fire in a clearing in the foothills. As he got nearer, there appeared to be a gathering of people chanting and dancing in a ring around the fire. Being curious, he ended up drifting a little lower than he should have, and was suddenly jerked into awareness of danger by a movement from the trees to the right of the fire. He climbed sharply, just as an arrow was released into the air, hurtling up towards him, just glancing his leg. The force sent him sideways for a moment before he recovered himself and pushed up higher and out of range. He was lucky it wasn't his wing because he could still fly, but he'd had to find a safe place to stop and rest until he knew he could manage to continue his journey to the mountains. Eventually, he made it there and left the container in a cavity in a rock. His return flight, though, had been really long and difficult.

"What can we do, Ryder? It looks like it might be broken."

"Sarah, ask him if we can carry him inside — we'll be very careful not to hurt him, but he needs us to take a look at his injury."

"He can understand you and he's okay with that. Ryder, keep your beak closed, okay?"

"Sarah, run ahead and clear one end of the table. Get a blanket from the box in the living room and put it on the table." Mary bent down and placed a hand firmly either side of his body, wings tucked in, and carried him inside, placing him down gently. Sarah stroked the soft feathers down his back while Mary fetched some warm water, cloths and bandages. "I wonder what we can use as a splint? How about you go into the mill room and see whether you can spot something like a small piece of wood? Two would be better." As Sarah ran off, Mary looked around the room. "Ryder, I'm not sure how to do this — it's too awkward getting at your injured leg while you're standing on the table and I don't expect you'd be very happy lying on your side, so I'm looking for a block that you can balance on with your good leg supporting you, while I tend to the other." Her eyes lit onto a small wooden box standing on the hearth. "Oh, that will do." She picked it up and returned to the table, placing it well in from the edge. She placed him on the box, waiting with one hand either side of his body until he gained his balance.

When Sarah returned with two narrow, flat pieces of wood, Mary left her keeping an eye on him while she went to the kitchen, returning with a small, heavy wooden mortar in which she'd mixed a paste of ginger and turmeric.

"They're natural pain relievers, so I'm going to wash his leg, smear the paste onto a small piece of cotton that I'll put around his injury, place a splint either side of his leg, then bind it all together with the bandage. It's not completely shattered, but it looks broken and it needs time to heal. I don't think bird legs take very long to heal, but we're going to have to try to keep him quiet for a good week."

Ryder squawked and Sarah laughed. "He says he's broken his leg, not his voice! Mary, do you think you could teach me, sometime, about natural healing? I brought some herbs and things from Morwyn's because they're fascinating. I've put them on the shelf in my room and I'd love to know more."

"My knowledge is fairly rudimentary, but I'm happy to share what I know. Morwyn was known for her healing, but it looks like she also used it for other purposes! Going back to what Ryder was saying about being shot, though — I've been thinking about it and it's really worrying. It seems to me that the people up there were up to something they needed a guard for, something like calling up magic, which is forbidden in North Feasgar. I wonder what's going on — we must tell Arthur later."

They were strapping on the outer bandage when they heard the sound of an approaching vehicle, wheels scrunching on the loose gravel of the driveway.

"Tom and Arthur are back," Sarah exclaimed, after checking and seeing the truck turning off the road. The next minute Tom charged through the door.

"Sarah, Arthur let me drive the truck the last stretch home. It's so cool — it's really...," his voice cut off abruptly as he noticed what they were both doing. "What's happened?" He raced over to the table and Sarah explained what had happened as they finished binding Ryder's leg.

"Now what? What does Ryder do with himself for the next week?"

"We keep him quiet, warm and comfortable, and don't let him get into any more trouble," responded Mary.

"But he can't just stay in one place for a week," objected Tom. "Hey, how about I make him a little cart thing he can sit on and push himself around with his good leg?"

Sarah just raised an eyebrow, "Well, good luck with that! Ryder says he'll be happy if we just put him down on the floor — he's quite capable of hopping around on his own!"

"So, what about his food? Hey, I know, Hermione can catch rats and mice for him. What do you say to that, Hermione?"

Hermione just sniffed and resumed her grooming, but they both knew she'd make sure Ryder was okay, even if she did let them know how much that would put her out!

By the time Arthur came into the house, Ryder was back on the floor and Tom had started talking about what it had been like going back to the treehouse and burying Morwyn's body. He was so glad for Arthur's presence — he made it all look different — much less scary and menacing, although that was maybe something to do with Morwyn no longer being a threat. As they ruminated on the past week, it seemed surreal to them all. So much packed into a few short days, and so different to their old lives. They scarcely felt like the same people. In the middle of a conversation between Sarah and Arthur, Tom suddenly burst in with a thought that had been playing on his mind.

"I've been thinking — maybe some of the lost children you hear about in the papers, the ones who stay missing, when they never find a body — maybe they're kids who've gone through a rift and end up here! Oh, and what I've been wanting to know too, is why the golden container is needed for the elixir? How come a kid couldn't be sent with any old container?"

"Well," said Arthur, trying to sound a bit mysterious, "The folklore of North Feasgar says that the honey has special healing properties just on its own, but when it's placed in the golden container, it's magically transformed into an elixir with rejuvenating properties. If a small amount is taken each year at Midsummer's Eve, it will create eternal life. We've always known the story, as a remnant of the old times before Feasgar was divided, but goodness only knows how and where Willard found it... I'm sure it wasn't by any legitimate means!"

There was a lull in the conversation and Mary nodded at Sarah. She swallowed, suddenly feeling really anxious and unsure of herself. She twisted her ponytail around and around her finger, tighter and tighter.

"Your finger will drop off if you're not careful," Tom noted.

"... Tom, there's a way back home if we want to take it..."

"What? How?" He looked perplexed, a frown creasing across his brow.

"I don't think you saw Morwyn's map — you were drugged, and I took it with me when I left the treehouse. It might still be in the pannier, but maybe I lost it — I can't recall seeing it for a while. Anyway, in the middle of the map there's a labyrinth that Morwyn didn't want me to ask questions about. She tried to make out that it was a bad place, but Mary tells me that if we go there, what's in the centre will reveal to us what we need to do — to stay or go back."

"I don't need to go there. I know that I'm never going back!" He stared at Sarah, eyes wide open and questioning. "What? You won't will you?"

"I don't know. I need to go to find out. I think I have some unfinished things to do in England with my family, and I think we need to go to the labyrinth together — we've been in this together so far, and I don't want to go there on my own. Will you come with me?"

Tom ran his hands nervously through his hair so that it stood up in dark tufts around his head. "But I've got used to you. You can't go!" It looked as if he may be about to cry.

"Tom, if I go, it won't be forever. I already know from what Mary's seen that I'll be coming back. I've got used to you too. I really like and trust you. But I need to do this, and I know you'll be okay. You'll have Mary and Arthur, and Hermione and Ryder. They all need you as much as you need them. Just think of all the things you can learn here and how much you can help them too."

Tom got up and ran out of the room and through the back door. Arthur followed after a few minutes and found him in the back garden, kicking distractedly at the pebbles on the path.

"Look," Arthur said gently, "Why don't you come back in and sit down and have a cup of tea while we talk to you about the labyrinth? Then you can decide whether you want to go with Sarah. I can tell she's pretty much made up her mind that she needs to go anyway, so all we can do is help her by making it as easy as possible for her. Have you heard the saying 'If you love something, let it go. If it comes back, it's yours forever, if it doesn't, then it was never meant to be'?"

Tom nodded silently.

"She'll come back and we need to make sure that she really wants to because of us, not just because she feels that she doesn't have a choice. I know it's hard, but we'll all be okay." He put his arm around Tom's shoulders and led him back inside.

Sitting back in the living room, Mary and Arthur explained what they understood about the labyrinth.

"The legends say that if you walk this labyrinth, being open to the sacredness and symbolism of it, then when you reach the centre, you'll find a rocky circle containing a pool of water. If you have the right attitude of receptiveness and respect, the water will be still, and gazing on it will reflect back to you what your inner strengths are and what you need to do to further your journey to wholeness. You may need to return several times over your lifetime at critical points where you seek guidance and direction. If you visit for the wrong reasons the surface will remain unsettled and perhaps, if you do see anything, it may be something you don't want to know! I imagine that's why Morwyn was afraid of it."

"When Mary and I went," Tom looked up, surprised at Arthur's words, "It was clear to us when we looked into the pool, that we couldn't go back. It was too late and our families had moved on. It was also clear that our paths lay here, in North Feasgar, and that we were needed here to support a young boy and girl who would appear in the future, that together we would embark on some perilous adventures of great importance. We think that refers to the two of you." They paused for a moment, with Tom and Sarah not being sure how to take it all in...

"But, if we need to go back, how do we do that?" Sarah asked.

"I don't know, but I'm sure it will become clear to you."

"But, how does it work?" demanded Tom. "None of it makes any sense..."

"Neither does you being here, does it? Not everything can be explained logically. Maybe it's about learning to trust your instincts and just letting things happen that feel right?" suggested Arthur.

"We can take you both to the labyrinth," Mary continued, "But we can't go in with you. It's your journey and you have to undertake it either on your own, or together, as two people who genuinely care about and want the best for each other, and somehow balance and complete each other."

"Oh, like the word Anam Cara?" said Sarah. "Soul friends. I read it in Morwyn's book and it felt so right that I brought it with me when we left the treehouse. So that's why you two went together."

Tom had a funny feeling starting up inside him. It suffused through his chest and down through his body, and up to his head. It felt warm and uplifting and made his eyes feel watery. He wasn't used to feeling good, or that he could trust people. Yet here were three people, and a cat and a bird, who had become so important to him, so quickly. He wondered if it was love he was feeling. It was a bit like the way he felt about his grandparents, minus all the anxiety that being at home enveloped him in and that stopped him from noticing his feelings, other than the bad ones he tried to escape from. It was a bit like a fog was lifting, and his feelings coming out were still a bit too bright and shiny for him to be comfortable with, but he knew deep down how much he yearned for them.

The rest of the day passed quickly. Tom and Sarah took turns keeping Ryder company, although he seemed happy in his makeshift bed on the floor, which consisted of a blanket and a bowl of water. Hermione went hunting for Ryder's dinner and the others quietly went about their chores around the house, slightly subdued and trying not to think about the next day.

Chapter XI
Walking the Labyrinth

Sarah woke to the morning of her eighth day in the land, with a feeling that was hard to work out. It was a feeling that something hugely important was about to happen, part excitement, part dread, part grief at probably leaving her new friends. It was a nervous and wobbly feeling, a bit like when she'd had to stand up at school assembly, and read the short story she'd won a prize for. Good and bad mashed up together. Opening her eyes, the first thing she saw was Hermione, pacing backwards and forwards across the room.

"Hermione, what is it?"

Hermione jumped up onto the bed. "I'm not sure. I can feel that something isn't right, though I've scouted around the house and there's nothing there. Maybe it's just that you'll be leaving, but I'm sure there's trouble brewing."

Sarah felt a prickle spread all over her skin and shivered. Hermione let her stroke her, but she couldn't relax again and slid out of the bed. She could hear Mary and Arthur moving around downstairs, and the soft murmuring of their voices as she gathered her clothes. She selected the ones she'd arrived in, freshly laundered. They'd talked last night about not knowing what the circumstances might be like on her return, whether she'd go back to the same place, or how she could explain away her absence if she needed to. It would be one less complication to at least arrive back looking the same — in these clothes, her hair untied. If her shoes looked a little more battered, she doubted anyone would notice.

She padded quietly down the corridor to the bathroom, had a wash and cleaned her teeth. Looking briefly into Tom's bedroom, she could see he was still asleep and she quietly closed the door, thinking that he didn't need any more worry today. She knew he was going to take her leaving really hard and he was likely to feel that she'd abandoned him. She hoped he'd changed enough already that he wouldn't have to cope by being angry and pretending she didn't matter, but she knew Arthur and Mary, and particularly Hermione, would help with that. Making her way downstairs to talk to them, she wondered again at how easy it was to already feel as if she belonged here. Was she doing the right thing? She felt torn, and knew all she could do was trust her intuition.

Mary and Arthur were in the kitchen. At the sight of Sarah, they drew apart as if they'd been talking about her, and Mary hurried over to her. "How are you feeling? I'll bet you're a bit confused and anxious about today." She touched her lightly on the arm as a gesture of concern.

"All sorts of things are going through my mind. I'm worried about leaving all of you, and what will happen when I get back to England. I feel sick with worry! And as well as that, Hermione is feeling unsettled. She thinks something is wrong, and I trust her instincts, and don't know what to do."

"What did she say?"

"Just that it feels like trouble's brewing, but she's checked around the mill and can't see anything. Oh look, here she is now. Have you spotted anything, Hermione?"

"No, everything seems quiet, but I think we need to leave here as soon as possible. Tom's just woken up."

*

Tom came downstairs a short time later to find a serious undertone to their conversation. As they sat to eat their breakfast, both he and Sarah became increasingly subdued as they struggled with their emotions. A heavy silence had settled on them, surrounding them in a bubble, withdrawn from the others, leaving them unable to communicate while they mechanically ate their food. An unknown stretched ahead of them, with change a reality neither wanted to face. Hermione suddenly jumped lightly up onto the table in front of them, arching her back.

"Right, you two, enough of that. Snap out of it — you need your wits about you today. Help Arthur clear the table while Mary checks on Ryder. You're leaving in ten minutes."

"What about you?" demanded Sarah.

"I've decided I need to stay here with Ryder. He's vulnerable at the moment and since we can't be sure where the sense of threat is coming from, we can't leave him alone."

Sarah swallowed and held back her tears as she started to clear the table. She felt a physical and emotional wrench even at the thought of saying goodbye to Hermione. When they were ready to leave, Sarah knelt down in front of Ryder and softly ran her index finger over the feathers on the back of his head and down his back, marvelling again at their beautifully complex and overlapping colours.

"Ryder, please get better soon. I'm going to miss you so

much. Thank you for being with me on that terrible journey down the river."

Ryder rubbed his beak against her hand. "I wouldn't have been able to if you hadn't rescued me! I'll still be here when you come back." He gave her a gentle nip that was to say *enough now*.

Sarah turned to Hermione, her eyes filling with tears that silently slid down her cheeks as she gathered her soft body to her in a last hug. She buried her face in her silky grey fur, feeling her warmth and hearing the rumble of her purr. She loved this cat and felt so in tune with her that leaving her was like wrenching away from part of herself. Hermione wriggled from her grasp, giving her a last pat on her cheek with a soft paw before leaping to the ground.

"You need to go now. Be safe and strong. If you face forward and trust your intuition, we'll meet again." She rubbed herself against Sarah's legs and bounded off out the door to check, once more, that all was well before they left.

Arthur had started the truck, so they left the house; Mary getting in beside Arthur, Sarah and Tom clambering onto the back. Once out on the road, Sarah watched Riverstone getting smaller and smaller until it was just a distant shape, feeling a jumble of emotions that left her stomach knotted and her heart heavy.

*

They were driving south from Riverstone, covering ground Tom and Sarah hadn't seen before. Tom looked around with interest as they drove past open countryside with a mixture of farm and agricultural small holdings, not dissimilar to some of the countryside where he came from. He noticed a vehicle in the distance behind them that was slowly gaining on them. It then settled into the same speed they were travelling, at what seemed to be a steady following distance. Tom's attention pricked up and he tried to study the vehicle more carefully. It was a car rather than a truck, but he couldn't make out any details.

It was when they turned off to the left into the road that he presumed led to the labyrinth, that he started to get edgy, because the car turned off too. Now, he was sure they were being followed. He told Sarah, who had been immersed in a world of her own since they left Riverstone, and banged on the window in the truck's cab. When Mary turned around to find out what was going on, he gesticulated to her until she understood what was happening and passed it on to Arthur. When he turned back to the road behind, the car had inched a little closer and he noticed, with a lurch in his stomach, that it looked like Morwyn's dusty green car. There couldn't be many more around like it. He grabbed Sarah's arm and they both watched in terror, imagining that somehow, she'd come back to life and was after them to get her revenge. How could that be? Was she more magical than they'd thought? Their hearts racing, Sarah rubbed her sticky palms down her tights, as Tom tried to tell Mary through the glass what they feared. He and Sarah looked at each other, Tom giving an uncertain smile of reassurance, but it didn't reach his eyes. Sarah licked her dry lips and dug her nails into her hands to stop them from shaking. Tom could feel sweat trickling down the side of his face from his forehead and impatiently wiped it away. He didn't want Sarah seeing his fear, but when she reached over and gripped his hand, he squeezed it, realising that they were in this together and were stronger together than apart.

The road began to curve a little as they drove through a copse of trees. As they rounded a bend to the left, Arthur suddenly swung the steering wheel sharply, pulling it off the road onto the bumpy verge. Turning off the motor, he and Mary jumped out of the truck.

"Quick, both of you, off the truck and over into those trees — now!"

They followed Arthur into the trees, where he indicated that Tom and Sarah must wait until they were called. He and Mary hunkered down on the edge of the trees watching the road. Shortly after, the green car drove around the bend, continuing along the road until the driver slowly registered that he, or she, had passed the stationary truck and slammed on the brakes. The car backed back towards them and stopped. The door opened and a tall, rangy, craggy man appeared.

"Willard!" breathed Mary.

As he walked towards the truck, Arthur put a hand on Mary's arm, clearly indicating that she was to remain hidden, then he stood and walked out to meet him.

"So, Willard, what are you doing following us?"

"Where's the container that girl stole from me?"

"Nowhere any of us can find it. It's been taken far away."

"I got a ride to Morwyn's turnoff yesterday and saw you and a boy drive out onto the main road. When I got to the treehouse it was deserted. Have you done something to Morwyn? It's very strange she's been so absent, though I'm guessing she was the one who told the girl about the container... bitch! I want a word with her, but even more I want the girl. Give her up to me and I'll leave the rest of you. I could see her and the boy on the back of your truck."

"Now, why would I do that?"

"Because you value your life." Willard was advancing on Arthur and reached down to flick a knife out from the inside of his boot. They circled each other warily, Willard with his knife arm outstretched and knees bent in a menacing pose; Arthur looking nimble and light on his feet, but unarmed. Willard parried with his knife, forcing Arthur to duck and dodge. He moved in closer.

Sarah and Tom had moved to the edge of the trees and were holding their breath in terror. Tom wondered briefly where Mary had gone, but his attention was pulled back to fix on Willard as he moved in suddenly to attack Arthur. Sarah gasped, but just then they heard a yell from the trees a little to their right and Mary charged out towards the two men brandishing a hefty tree branch. Willard lost his focus for a second as he looked towards the disturbance, just enough time for Arthur to kick out hard at his groin. He doubled over, striking out at the same time with his knife. Mary brought the branch down hard on his arm, knocking away the knife and making Willard grunt with pain. She then lifted the branch again and brought it down hard across his shoulders and neck.

"Oommph." All the air was knocked out of him as he collapsed and hit the ground hard. He appeared to have been knocked out. Tom and Sarah raced out from their cover in time to see Mary run over to where Arthur was slumped on the ground, holding his arm, which was streaming with blood.

"Quick, Sarah, go to the glovebox of the truck and bring the windscreen cloths. Tom, get the rope from the back of the truck and tie Willard's hands behind his back." As she spoke, she was lying Arthur down properly on the ground and elevating his arm. When Sarah brought her the cloths, she rolled one and tied it tightly above the long knife wound that ran down the outside of his arm. The second cloth she pressed hard against the wound, wondering what she could use to pad the wound before she bound it.

"Are you all right, Tom?" she asked after a while, glancing over to where he was attempting to knot the rope around Willard's wrists.

"Yeah, but I don't know how tight to make it."

"Sarah, press here while I help Tom and look for something for Arthur's arm."

Sarah pressed down on the cloth, as Mary moved over to Willard and pulled tightly on the rope Tom had wound around his wrists. She then took the loose end and tied it round his ankles behind his back. Willard groaned.

"Don't expect any mercy from me, you piece of dirt! You've held me at knife point, you abducted us and kept us captive for weeks, and now you've attacked Arthur." She yanked at the rope even harder, tying it off with an impressive looking knot. He wasn't going to get free any time soon!

She then ran into the trees, emerging again a few minutes later with some fabric in her hands. She knelt down beside Arthur, who raised an eyebrow at her.

"Is that…?"

"Yes, it is. Don't you say anything. I always thought there

had to be a better use for such a silly contraption," she said, as she pressed her padded bra linings against the knife wound, tying them on firmly with the last of the cloths from the truck. She and Sarah then helped him up into a sitting position, looking pale, with an unhealthy sheen on his skin, but still very much alive.

Willard, meanwhile, had roused himself enough to roll awkwardly onto his side. As Arthur was helped to his feet, Willard mumbled, "What are you going to do with me?"

"Leave you, that's what! It's going to be a long way back for you, trussed up like that!" Arthur walked over to him and, seeing Willard trying to roll away to get on his knees, gave him a push with his foot to make him lose his balance and fall back to the ground.

"Don't you ever," he continued forcefully, "come near any of us again, or you might not get away with your life! Tom, do you think you can drive the truck? I think we might take Morwyn's car as well just so Willard can appreciate a good walk. Mary can drive with Sarah and I'll go with you."

He then untied the rope round Willard's ankles, leaving Willard looking twisted and dishevelled on the ground. They went to the vehicles and two in each, drove off. Arthur guided Tom to drive the truck ahead of the car, while Mary followed. As they left Willard behind, Sarah let out a long breath. It felt as if she'd been holding it ever since she saw Morwyn's car behind them on the road. She still felt shaky, like she'd just run a long race, pushing herself too hard — her chest was tight and her knees wobbly. Mary reached over to her and put her hand on her arm.

"Well, that was pretty awful, wasn't it? You and Tom did really well. Arthur will be all right, and now you need to leave it behind you so that you can focus on the labyrinth."

"Tell me about it please, Mary. What's it like?"

"It's hard to describe — it isn't what it appears to be, it's much more complex. It's more about what you experience."

"What do you mean?"

"Physically it is a very large stone circle with inner walls that guide you in a unicursal way to the centre."

"What's unicursal?"

"It means there is only one way to the centre. It's different to a maze — with a maze you have to solve a puzzle about how to get to the centre and it's possible to get completely lost — especially with those hedge ones that are very high, blocking out any way of seeing where you are. A labyrinth is designed to provide a path to the centre that you can use to walk in a contemplative frame of mind, giving you a chance to reflect on your life and what's important to you. Have you seen one before?"

"No, but in England there's one at Hilton, near Cambridge, where my grandparents lived for a while. It's called a maze, but my grandmother says it's actually a labyrinth. They used to go there quite a lot. It's made of turf."

"Well, this one is made of stone, which is about waist height. I'm not sure when it was built, but it feels very old. When you enter, you have to turn left, and by following the curves you're guided through to the middle. You'll constantly be turning and will lose your sense of direction, but if you keep open to it rather than anxious, and trust that you'll get to the centre, it's really relaxing. The weird thing is that the stone only comes to your waist, so in theory you can see over it towards the centre and not lose your bearings, but there must be something magical still working in the labyrinth, because if you look up, your attention just slides off, back to the path. It's like it's impossible to find your way to the centre any other way than by walking its meandering direction."

While they'd been talking, the landscape had started to change. The gently rolling land and trees had given way to low growing, scrubby bushes on a flat plain that reminded her of the moors in England. The road began to straighten out, to which Tom breathed a sigh of relief. It was exciting getting to drive the truck, but it took all his attention and was draining. He was still feeling edgy after the wrangle with Willard. His nerves were frayed and he was perched on the edge of the driver's seat still feeling the adrenalin in his body. As focusing on the road became easier, he relaxed back a little and lifted his head from the patch of road immediately ahead to look at his surroundings. As he gazed from side to side, he could see that the road had started to slope slightly down towards a central plateau, a pattern repeated in all directions around him. It was as if he was driving along the spoke of a wheel, heading towards the hub. He wondered how this landscape had formed — he'd always been interested in geology — he was meant to be taking geography at school this year, if he ever got back there. He stopped himself from this train of thought. Now wasn't the time for wondering — he needed to focus on where he was now.

Looking in his rear-view mirror he could see Morwyn's car a little behind, with Sarah in the front looking around at the countryside.

"Tom, you're doing great," said Arthur. "I'm really proud of you. It's not far now."

Tom swallowed, unused to a male saying positive things to him. A short time later they arrived at the end of the road, and faced a large stone circle. Arthur directed him to turn right into the road that ran around the labyrinth. About twenty metres later they came to a section of flattened dirt to the right of the road, opposite an opening in the stone wall. Arthur indicated that he should park there, so Tom pulled the truck off the road and parked it, with Mary driving Morwyn's car in behind, pulling up beside them. Getting out of the truck, Tom's hands felt clammy and he was suddenly very nervous. This was it then. The decision point. After only a bit more than a week in this land, it felt like they'd been here forever and it felt quite surreal that they could even be considering leaving it. He knew in his heart, though, that whatever happened, he would *never* go back to his mum and Gerald.

The four of them stood facing each other.

"I don't know what to say," said Mary, "Other than that what is meant to happen will happen. Please remember that you'll always have a place to stay with us. It feels as if we've known you for so long already, as if we're meant to be together."

She told them that they would leave the truck and go back to Riverstone in the car to bind Arthur's arm properly, and they would be back in about an hour to wait for them. They would wait for two hours, and if they didn't emerge from the labyrinth they would return home, but would come back again the next day to check.

They hugged them both with a warm and heartfelt embrace, not wanting to let them go. Mary had tears in her eyes, and Arthur told them, with a break in his voice, that it was time for them to go, and to approach the labyrinth with openness. Tom and Sarah looked at each other, both overwhelmed with their feelings for Mary and Arthur. It was almost impossible to move away from them to cross the road. Tom took a deep breath and held out his hand to Sarah, who took it silently. With heavy hearts and yet a strange feeling of calm, knowing that they had at last reached some sort of threshold that they needed to cross, they smiled at Mary and Arthur and walked together across the road and into the entrance to the labyrinth.

They didn't look back. The stone walls directed them to their left, and as they turned, a hush fell on them. They were enveloped in a strange stillness, as if they were suddenly breathing different air. Hand in hand they set off on their circuitous journey to the centre. Tom tried to look over the stone wall to see how large it was, and how far it was to the centre, but weirdly his eyes couldn't fix on anything, other than the path in front. He tried and tried, starting to get agitated, until Sarah said, "Tom, don't. Mary told me this would happen. It's part of the magic of the place. Stop and take a deep breath. We need to walk on with open hearts and minds. It's something about the journey and what we experience together that will make sure we're okay with whatever happens."

Tom nodded, standing still for a few moments, breathing deeply from the still air.

"Here, hold my hand again, another deep breath... now let's walk quietly and let our minds wander over what brought us here, what's happened, how we feel now and where we want to be in the future. Don't try to think it, just let your mind relax and see what happens." She realised this was probably easier for her, happy in trusting her intuition and imagination. But Tom had come so far — she knew he could do it.

It was like a slow meandering that had its own rhythm. Quiet steps, footfalls muffled by the packed earth, curves leading first one direction, then another, ever heading towards the centre. They were separate and yet together in their memories and thoughts. At the same time, they were present to a sense of deep gratitude for the changes their experiences had brought about in them, and for the warmth and love offered by the incredible people (and Hermione and Ryder!) they had met. And, they both acknowledged to themselves the importance of having each other to share it with. Their progress started with remembering, but somehow drifted into letting all their fears go, being able to receive love and find themselves open to the future. It was calming and soothing — for a while, the outside world ceased to exist as they walked, their attention turned inward, while at the same time anchored to each other.

They lost all track of time. It may have taken fifteen minutes, or maybe an hour. Eventually, in a calm and dream-like state, they reached an opening that led into the inner circle of the labyrinth. There they found a natural looking rocky platform, with a raised central piece, shaped a bit like an irregular basin. Around the platform, strangely, exotic, unusual plants neither of them had seen before were growing, making it look like some sort of tropical spa, even though the ground since they entered the labyrinth had been barren — just packed earth and dust. They could hear the sound of water and could only imagine that the pond they sought was in the raised basin, and its water supply was creating the beautiful oasis they could see. Silently they approached, finding stones placed to lead them up onto the platform. Once there, they found themselves gazing down at a pool of water, still and deep and clear. The sound they could hear came from somewhere down below the ground — the surface of the pool was as still as a mirror, reflecting the blue sky and tufts of white cloud.

As Sarah had walked, she had come more clearly to the resolution that she needed to go back. She needed to see her parents and make sure they were okay, without wanting to fix things for them. She needed to find out how she could be in the world with all the things she'd experienced and learned — whether it could be different, whether she could be different, although she already knew the answer to that. As she gazed on the surface of the water, a slight wind ruffled the surface for a second, then as it cleared, she realised she could see her parents and grandparents. Her mother was crying, her father had his arm around her shoulders. The surface rippled again, clearing to show her Tom, looking a little older, and the Birches. There were storm clouds gathering in the background, but they looked content and were gazing into the distance, obviously waiting for something or someone. Maybe waiting for her?

Tom knew he would never go back. As he gazed on the surface he saw the mill house, the Birches, Hermione and Ryder. They were working hard in the garden, but he could feel their love and acceptance radiating out from the image. Sarah wasn't there. Would she come back? Hermione had told him that she would when the time was right, when they really needed her. As he looked again, he caught a glimpse of Gerald and his mother, in the kitchen, his mother looking miserable and Gerald sitting, waiting for her to serve him his dinner. Leah was nowhere to be seen. This wasn't his future. He turned to Sarah and saw her resolve reflected in her eyes. He tried to speak and couldn't find any words. Tears came to his eyes and Sarah reached for him and they hugged each other, the soft flutter of their hearts joining for a moment before Sarah pulled away.

"Tom, I don't know how to say how much you've come to mean to me. I have to go, but I know I'll be back." Knowing now what she had to do, she took a final look at him, gave a half smile, climbed up onto the edge of the basin and dived swiftly and cleanly into the pool. Down and down she plunged. The water was cool and smooth, almost oily on her skin, gentle, soothing and embracing. She slid through the water, gliding effortlessly, weightlessly, luxuriously. She rolled and turned, experimenting with the freedom she felt, and it was as if she could breathe and be one with the water, and was dissolving into millions of tiny bubbles...

Chapter XII
Sarah's Return

She opened her eyes and saw her grandfather smiling at her.

"Well, you had us worried, sleepy-head. You've been asleep for so long that we were beginning to wonder whether you'd come back to us."

The worried faces of her parents were suddenly behind him, and the room was somewhere she didn't recognise. As her eyes became accustomed to being open, she looked around and saw that she was in a hospital room, with windows on her left and monitors and a drip-stand to her right. Her mum came over closer to her and held her hand, her eyes looking moist and a little red-rimmed.

"Can you remember what happened, darling? Gran found you asleep in the living room in front of the fire, and you wouldn't wake up. You've been in a coma for more than a week. The doctors don't know what happened — you haven't bumped your head or anything. We've all been so worried."

Her father slid into view, putting his hand on her mother's shoulder. "Hello, peanut, we're very glad to see you awake again. You gave us such a fright." He took her other hand, and as she fell into an exhausted sleep, she smiled, thinking that clearly some things had changed already.

A Jungian perspective for the older reader

When I first thought about writing this book, I wanted to write more than an exciting story for younger adults to read. I was keen for the reader to learn a little about themselves and the ways they react and behave. As a Jungian analyst, I naturally lean towards Carl Jung's approach to depth psychology, and it is this that has guided my writing.

This tale uses allegory to illustrate the psychological tasks that a person may need to undertake in order to find a sense of wholeness. Before unpacking what that means, a short introduction to the work of Carl Jung is needed. Jung founded a field of psychology known as analytical psychology, which holds at its core that in order to become a whole person, we need to bring together our conscious sense of who we are in the world (called our ego consciousness) and that part of us our ego has no control over (called our unconscious) into a relationship, which leads to what Jung called 'individuation'. This helps us to make meaning out of our lives, bringing with it the possibility of becoming who we have the potential to be, rather than being defined by our past experiences. Jung defines individuation as being to "denote the process by which a person becomes 'in-dividual', that is a separate, indivisible unity or 'whole'."[2]

While some people prefer to live their lives without an appreciation of the influence of their unconscious, others value self-development, and the attempt to understand their unconscious motivations and behaviour in order to become more balanced and whole. Regardless, throughout our lives we will be confronted with psychological challenges, such as those faced by Sarah and Tom. Choosing to attempt to resolve these challenges may determine whether we can free ourselves from emotional states that grip us, and behaviours that we later regret. Dealing with these challenges also determines whether we can live our lives with a sense of fulfilment and generativity, or whether life becomes something we have to suffer and survive.

The tale begins with two young people from opposite sides of the world being abandoned in different ways by their parents, and being thrown together. Jung maintains that each of us, male or female, has an inner aspect of the opposite gender that we need to develop for balance. That is, a male has a feminine aspect in his psyche called his anima, and a female a masculine aspect called her animus. The use of the terms masculine and feminine don't equate to 'male' or 'female' in physical terms, but as an inner psychic balance to whatever gender we identify with in the external world as we strive for wholeness. This involves a deepening that is about finding 'soul'. The book series has therefore been titled 'The Anam Cara Triology', with the word anamchara, or anam cara (pronounced *anahm karuh*) being an old Celtic word from the Ogham language, meaning 'soul friend' or the experience of 'compassionate presence'.[1]

Sarah and Tom set out together to learn about, and support, each other, through the tasks they need to complete for self-development, much as Hänsel and Gretel journey together in the Grimms' fairytale. Hänsel and Gretel is about abandonment; about parents who either physically or emotionally abandon their children, the consequent long-term effects on them, and the tasks they may need to face in a journey to recovery and individuation. There is always a degree of ambivalence associated with being a parent, brought about by the requirements of caring for children sometimes being at odds with the immediate interests of their own; the natural desire to be selfish versus the self-sacrifice needed for protecting and preserving the species. This is a dilemma all parents face, yet many do not acknowledge. The fairy-tale of Hänsel and Gretel, and our story, draw attention to the abandoning impulse in parents, which, if acted out, will have a devastating effect on the child.

Tom needs to learn about relationship and trust. While he is active in their adventures, his major task in this tale is to confront the 'terrible mother' within, illustrated by the figure of Morwyn in the story, or by the witch in Hänsel and Gretel. He also has to learn about waiting, patience and being able to be still; deeply feminine qualities (in a psychological sense). Sarah needs to find an inner strength to take her through the tasks of differentiating or sorting; of using her wit to confront the negative masculine in the form of Willard, to obtain what she needs to save Tom; and to focus and be satisfied. This latter task is something that is perhaps increasingly difficult in our rapidly evolving world of social media, where it is easy to become overwhelmed with possibilities, and to fragment parts of ourselves by sending little pieces constantly out into the world.

Morwyn has been created to form an example of the ambivalent feminine. She can be kind to the children when it suits her purpose — this contrasts with their experience of her as manipulative and nasty. Inconsistency is one of the hardest things for children to bear because they can't work out their defence strategies based on expected behaviour, and they can't always trust their perception — what if they've got it wrong? If they've been subjected to inconsistent behaviour from infancy, they learn how to adapt to cruel behaviour to make sure they get some form of affection and attention, even if to other people it 'looks like' abuse. While this aspect isn't part of this particular story, many children experiencing the influence of the negative feminine from childhood are manipulated to think it's all their fault and that they are the ones who have to adapt if they want to get love. Many grow up believing they're unlovable.

So, was it part of Morwyn's purpose to treat them as she did to help them to 'grow', or was it all about getting what she wanted by manipulative means? This remains unclear in the story, which alludes to the ambivalent outcomes of our experiences of pain and suffering. Often, if we allow ourselves to unpack these experiences and make meaning from them, they help us to deepen and mature in a way that wouldn't otherwise have occurred. Yet their experiences were undeniably not something to be wished for. The experience with Morwyn was formative, but she was motivated by personal desire, without giving heed to the children's suffering.

This also draws attention to Morwyn's narcissism — the children had to be and do as she wanted, because the fulfilment of her desires was the only thing that mattered. How difficult it is for children when their mother or father can't see them as individuals, only as an extension of themselves and what they want. If their children don't fulfil their needs, they are often made to be invisible, that is, ignored, or cast away physically or metaphorically.

Morwyn's seeking of the elixir represents her desperate desire for physical perfection and fear of dying. The glimpse we get of her childhood shows the effects of transgenerational patterns and trauma, that in her case have resulted in narcissistic wounding. This sort of wounding means that she suffered such a profound sense of shame that she can't ever feel good about herself again, and has to act in ways that make her think that she is better than those around her. That the nectar comes from the narcissus flower, draws attention to the narcissistic dynamic. Readers may want to read Ovid's tale of Narcissus and Echo,[3,4] where this dynamic can be seen, along with the narcissist's need to have an echo to confirm their fragile sense of who they are. For this reason, a narcissistic woman often chooses a passive partner who will do as she wants, and turns most of her fury onto an eldest daughter. While narcissism obviously isn't gender bound, this particular mix is thought to be one of the more damaging family dynamics.[5]

While they must confront and overcome the negative masculine and feminine personified by Morwyn and Willard, Sarah and Tom find help through the opposite qualities. That is, the positive masculine and feminine in the guise of Ryder and Hermione, and later from the miller and his wife, Arthur and Mary, who Sarah rescues from Willard. Note, Tom chose Hermione's name from his projection onto the magical feminine character from Harry Potter, while Sarah chose the name Ryder for its representation of a knight or mounted warrior from the old English word 'rīdere'.

We can also see that Tom and Sarah have different personality types that complement each other. Jung proposed the theory of personality types that forms the basis for the Myers Briggs Type Inventory (MBTI), which is used in a wide range of contemporary applications. The MBTI proposes that of our four cognitive functions (Sensing, Intuition, Thinking and Feeling), while we use all of them, one of them will be our dominant function (the one we prefer to use and will use most naturally, like our dominant hand); one will be our inferior function (the one least developed and the clumsiest, like our non-dominant hand); and the other two will have a level of maturity somewhere in between, depending on our experiences and opportunities to develop them. Normally, one of these will work well with our dominant function to support it.

In our story, Tom and Sarah have contrasting dominant and auxiliary functions, which serve to highlight their differences, sometimes creating tension and conflict, and also creating the opportunity for them to support each other in a complementary fashion. They learn that no one way of being in the world is 'right' and that working together is more beneficial to them than working alone. While Tom likes to navigate his way in the world in a rational and carefully thought-out manner (Sensing and Thinking), he finds the imaginary, nebulous world into which he has plunged, particularly challenging. He also struggles to name and express his feelings. Sarah is more comfortable in a world of what seems to be a fictional surrounding with subliminal connections and relationships (Intuition and Feeling). They both learn a lot about their strengths and limitations, and to be able to depend on each other. In this way, they both become more integrated and whole, a task all of us confront if we are willing to go there.

Every individual or collective grouping (e.g. society, culture or religion) has a shadow that consists of all the aspects of 'other' that we don't want to be. On an individual level, that might be parts of our personality we don't like; fearful memories we don't want to remember; or aspects that influential people like our parents don't want us to be, maybe our sexuality, maybe our anger... We push these down into our unconscious, where they sit, cut off from our conscious ego, and percolate. Robert Bly[6] conceptualises this as the bag we carry behind us, getting heavier and heavier as we spend half a lifetime filling it up, and the other half trying to find out how to empty it. It gains energy if we ignore it, which leaves us less and less energy to draw on in our lives. He maintains that every part of our personality that we don't love becomes hostile to us, and if we distance it too greatly, it may revolt.

Our challenge is to turn to face our shadow and start to look at it, a little bit at a time. We need to cast some light on it so that it doesn't gain so much energy that it breaks out, either projected onto other people we dislike, or affecting us somatically through illnesses, classically things like irritable bowel syndrome or eruptive skin conditions. As Bly[6] writes, the substance locked up in the bag will appear one day *somewhere else*. Facing our shadow takes courage and good support, but the payoff is also immense, allowing us to lighten the load the bag places on us, with freed up psychic energy and a more self-aware, balanced and authentic life.

In our story, the southern land, cut off from North Feasgar, where the action takes place, represents the shadow (Note, Feasgar means the transitional time between day and night). The southern land has been completely severed from the north, but we need to remember that no one, and no group of people, can ever be 'only good'. We ignore the shadow at our peril. Not all of the things in our shadow are 'bad' even when we label them as such, so we cut off aspects of ourselves that could be useful to us, and could help us to become more understanding and three-dimensional. The energy of South Feasgar is getting stronger, while the north is only able to grow in a limited fashion. At some point (maybe in a future story?) the dark will break through and cause havoc for people ill-equipped to deal with it. Again, this happens to us as individuals when we don't try to develop self-awareness. Think of all the mid-life crises, depressions and anxieties in the world and the part this might play. Think too, on a collective level, of countries or religions that split themselves off as good and make anything outside that system 'bad'. It is easy to see how this drives a festering underworld that has to remain hidden and unacknowledged, while all those cast as 'other' can be treated as scapegoats and receive collective hatred or fear.

A labyrinth is an ancient symbol that relates to wholeness, and combines the imagery of the circle and the spiral in a meandering, but purposeful path. Sarah and Tom's adventures lead them to the centre of the land (the still point, the centre of themselves, as eloquently described in T. S. Eliot's poem included at the beginning of this book; or the Self as conceptualised by Jung), where they find the labyrinth. Following the path of the labyrinth is symbolic of our journey to our own centre and back again into the world. While in the labyrinth we are never truly lost, but at the same time we can't see where we are going. In this way it is different to a maze, which is a puzzle that needs to be solved. Instead, a labyrinth represents a sacred journey, giving us the opportunity to consider what is important to us as we travel to the centre, which could also be symbolised by a mandala. We need to be receptive and present to the experience, and to trust the twists and turns of the path we need to follow. Jung defines wholeness as the fullest possible expression of all aspects of our personality; in itself, in relation to other people and to the environment.[7] For Jung, this is equated with health, both as a potential and a capacity.

After successfully navigating the labyrinth, Tom and Sarah are given a choice. While Sarah chooses to return home, this isn't the end of the tale for her, as there is a major hurdle for her yet to achieve, that is, the feminine descent into the underworld. Tom remains; not alone, as he keeps with him their trusty companions, Ryder and Hermione. His journey is also incomplete. He has yet to safely cross the water (the unconscious) to find his sense of wholeness and to be reunited with Sarah. Together they will, at some point, need to confront the rising shadow represented by the dark forces of South Feasgar.

For examples of tales of self-development, you could read:

For the feminine: the myths of Psyche or Persephone; the book 'She' written by Robert Johnstone; or the many tales told by Clarissa Pinkola Estes (e.g. 'Women who run with the wolves'). For tales of the feminine descent to come, see these same myths; or the story of Innana and Ereshkigal.

For the masculine: the myth of Perseus; the fairytale of Hänsel and Gretel; the book 'He' written by Robert Johnstone; or 'Iron John' written by Robert Bly.

For facing the shadow: 'A Wizard of Earthsea' written by Ursula Le Guin.

References

O'Donohue, J. (1997). Anam Cara: A book of Celtic wisdom. New York: Harper Collins.

Jung, C. (1968b). The archetypes and the collective unconscious. (2nd Ed). Collected Works of C.G. Jung Volume 9, Part 1. New York: Princeton University Press.

Ovid's metamorphoses: Narcissus and Echo. (n.d.) Retrieved from: http://hompi.sogang.ac.kr/anthony/Classics/OvidEchoNarcissus.htm 1 May, 2018.

Greek Myths & Greek Mythology (2018). Retrieved from: https://www.greekmyths-greekmythology.com/narcissus-myth-echo/ 1 May, 2018 (for an interpretation of the myth).

McBride, K. (2008). Will I ever be good enough? New York: Atria Paperback.

Bly, R. (1988). A little book on the human shadow. New York: Harper Collins.

Samuels, A., Shorter, B., & Plaut, F. (1986). A critical dictionary of Jungian analysis. New York: Routledge & Kegan Paul Ltd.